Rijzen - Text copyright © Emmy Ellis 2024
Cover Art by Emmy Ellis @ studioenp.com © 2024

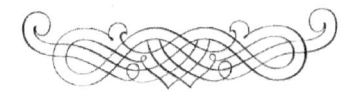

All Rights Reserved

Rijzen is a work of fiction. All characters, places, and events are from the author's imagination. Any resemblance to persons, living or dead, events or places is purely coincidental.

The author respectfully recognises the use of any and all trademarks.

With the exception of quotes used in reviews, this book may not be reproduced or used in whole or in part by any means existing without written permission from the author.

Warning: The unauthorised reproduction or distribution of this copyrighted work is illegal. No part of this book may be scanned, uploaded, or distributed via the Internet or any other means, electronic or print, without the author's written permission.

RIJZEN

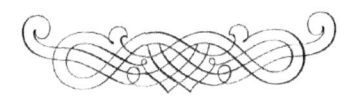

Emmy Ellis

Dedication

For Lynn Callow

Chapter One

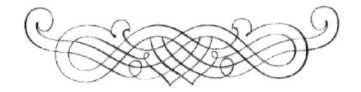

Moon had been let out of his room. Middle-aged Bart, one of the Amsterdam heavies, walked behind him down the stairs, his gun poking into Moon's shoulder. At the bottom, a man in a suit stood, *his* gun on prominent display. Menace. A warning. Nothing Moon wouldn't have ordered back in London. To be on the receiving end of such a thing got his goat. Now he understood how his pawns and victims felt. But there was a difference. He didn't treat anyone like shit unless they deserved it.

Maybe the Amsterdam boss thought he deserved it, but Moon didn't feel this treatment was justified. He also didn't feel anyone had the right to force him to do what they wanted. All right, *he'd* forced many people in his lifetime, but...

Ah bollocks, there was no getting out of it: he'd been a bully, too, he'd been just as unfair, and he had to face that fact without making excuses.

It was fucking difficult admitting you were wrong. That you were just as much of a bastard as all the men here.

Hendrik Alderliesten had, on the first visit, asked Moon to run some Dutch girls in the UK. Moon had refused, thinking of his missus, Debbie, and how she'd had to sell herself to eat and pay the rent. What Hendrik had proposed wasn't the same as the outfit Debbie ran in the East End, where all the girls were safe and protected. No, this bastard was running a trafficking ring and wanted Moon to be their pimp. He'd lied to the women, saying they'd have a good life, when in fact, they'd basically be prisoners, held in properties belonging to Moon, which was a bit rich, Hendrik expecting him to provide accommodation. They'd been rounded up and were currently held somewhere, probably scared out of their minds.

I should never have come back for a second visit. Should have phoned the police here and told them what was going on.

How often had he said that to himself while locked upstairs? Too often. When he'd arrived this time, it wasn't the fun and games he'd had before, high as a kite on weed and booze, Hendrik buttering him up. The bloke had repeated his offer, and when Moon had refused again, he'd been taken upstairs. Kept there. Bart bringing him food and water. What, as a way to drag Moon down until he accepted the job?

In the end, he had—but he had no plans to run those girls. He'd set them free. But before that, he'd take Hendrik down.

The twins were on their way.

He had nothing nice to say about this building in a deserted backstreet. Austere, no home comforts. A place for Hendrik to conduct business, to hide people away who wouldn't behave, nothing more. Moon imagined the tosser lived in a swanky house somewhere along the canal, a far cry from this shithole.

Where were the girls kept?

He'd strolled the main Red Light District that initial visit, all those lights, all those people, the 'coffee shops' where you could smoke weed like cigarettes, the purple glow from inside alerting passersby as to what was on offer. He'd been to Amsterdam in his younger years, too, and his first return as a mature man had been much of him reliving his youth, safe in the knowledge his Estate was in good hands with Alien and Brickhouse, the twins on standby if they were needed. He'd stayed away too long, enjoying himself too much, and as for coming back again, knowing what Hendrik wanted from him…

Madness. Stupidity. He'd thought he could persuade Hendrik to stop this nonsense, but it hadn't turned out that way.

"Best behaviour," Bart warned and opened the door to what would once have been a living room.

Moon stepped inside, familiar with it. This was where they'd initially chatted about the 'business proposition'. Hendrik sat behind a scabby old table, ten mismatched chairs around it. The man ought to be ashamed of himself, entertaining alliances in here. Moon treated his colleagues, for want of a better word, with respect, taking them to the finest restaurants on his Estate and sometimes Up West, depending on who he aimed to impress or get on his side. Hendrik? A fucking cheapskate, providing microwave meals and tap water in plastic cups.

"Sit," Hendrik said.

In the shadows of the corners, three men stood bearing weapons. None were as big as Moon's right-hand blokes, but they had an air about them, like Ichabod—probably ninja experts—where it was obvious you didn't want to mess with them. Normally they wouldn't bother him, but he was on his own here, no backup.

Moon sat opposite Hendrik. He supposed he was meant to apologise for refusing the offer a second time, to plead, to say he'd behave now, but fuck that. Showing this cock-nosed wanker any signs of weakness wasn't in his repertoire. He'd remain who he was, see how things went, although he *would* have to acquiesce and toe the line in order to get out of here.

"You've had a change of heart." Hendrik sipped from a cut-crystal glass. Whisky or brandy. He stroked a steel cigarette case on the table, leaving smudged fingerprints.

Moon would kill for a smoke. He hadn't had a cigar in ages. He'd also like to burn the ends of Hendrik's fingers, cut his hands off, slice his bastard throat.

"I have," Moon said. "Had time to think, didn't I. What you said makes sense. The girls will fit well on my Estate. Daft of me to have thought otherwise."

"How can I trust you now? You were so stubborn in your refusal—twice. Didn't you say you couldn't be budged? I might think you're agreeing to this just so I'll let you go."

"I'd think the same in your shoes, to be fair, so you'll have to take a punt on whether you believe me or not." Moon shrugged. "But if I don't go home soon, people will begin to wonder why I'm not bothered about leaving my Estate for so long."

"We've used your phone to speak to this Alien, Brickhouse, and Debbie. They're your most-used contacts so must mean something to you, hence why I chose them. They think you're having a great time."

Moon stopped himself from frowning. When Bart had left his room door open earlier, Moon had crept along the landing into an office of sorts and found his mobile in a desk drawer. He'd messaged Debbie, telling her he was trapped and to alert the twins, but there hadn't been any other sent messages on there. This lot must have deleted them.

"Yeah, but that will only fly so far." Moon eyed the alcohol. "And what about my hotel? I booked an open-ended stay, but my stuff…"

"Your room is still yours, your things are still there."

Moon had a vision of them going there, using his keycard, poking around. In his things. Better not to dwell, to antagonise them. "So are we going to drink to an allegiance or what?"

Hendrik nodded. "Yes, but only after you do something for me. I want proof you're not going to renege on the agreement."

Here we go. He's taken a leaf out of the leader book but hasn't quite got his delivery right. He's not scaring me like he should. Still, what the hell do I care so long as I get out of here?

"What do you need me to do?"

"Kill someone."

Moon barked laughter. "Is that all?" *Fuck. Fucking fuck.* Killing here was different to at home, where he was protected, knew the score, what he could and couldn't get away with. Nevertheless, he'd have to go along with this. Make out he didn't care. That this was just business. "Who is it?"

"You'll find out. Go with Bart."

Moon stood, casually walking to the door where Bart waited. He followed the bloke into the short hallway, bypassing the crabby-looking fella at the bottom of the stairs who clutched his gun a bit tighter.

Ponce.

Out in the backstreet, Moon sucked in the first breath of fresh air he'd had in a while. His liberty, although under the strict supervision of Bart, was welcome. What was the plan? He killed someone then was brought back here? Was Bart going to stand there and watch to make sure he did it? Video it?

Moon's mind raced. He could bolt, disappear into the maze of streets on this housing estate. Ask some random to phone the police—most people spoke English here, so communication wouldn't be a problem. But who knew if Hendrik had coppers in his pocket? Besides, he reckoned Bart would find him before he even reached anyone. No, it was better to act as though he was happy to do whatever they asked.

"Come with me," Bart ordered and turned into an alley.

Moon prepared himself to get the shit kicked out of him. The old ticker stalled for a second — he wasn't as young as he used to be and tended to use his men to do any dirty work, but he could still defend himself with his fists if he had to.

Not against a gun, though.

He entered the alley, expecting to find several men ready to ambush him, but only Bart's silhouette was in evidence, heading towards the other end where light from a streetlamp shone. This area wasn't near the streams of tourists who filled the city centre. Slotervaart was a neighbourhood, like an Estate where Hendrik had his base in a run-down street of what seemed like empty, abandoned homes.

Moon looked over his shoulder. The crabby man blocked his escape route. He could tell it was him by the shape of his hair, the slope of his shoulders, his wide-legged stance.

"Fuck's sake," Moon muttered and walked forward.

Bart waited at an SUV, holding the rear door open. "Get in."

Moon obeyed, casting a glance around the interior. Just your average vehicle. The driver, a young bloke with scraggly hair, someone he hadn't seen before, eyed him in the rearview. Moon eyed him back and judged him easy to take down if needed. But with Bart added to the mix, Moon had no chance.

Stop thinking of ways to escape and just accept the situation for what it is.

Who was this kid? Moon had counted six men in total every time he'd got together with Hendrik. Even when they'd gone out in the city the entourage had tagged along, as though Hendrik were a star and needed protection. Or maybe he needed to *feel* like a star—that was interesting; it gave an insight into who Hendrik was, someone who wanted to be important but might not be. Yes, there were guns and whatnot, and his outfit *looked* impressive, but what if it was all an illusion? What if Hendrik had been studying what went on in London, how there were leaders, and he'd tried to replicate that here?

That must be how he heard about me. Why he made contact and asked me to come over. He made me think he's some big hotshot, but what if he isn't?

That changes things.

A little of Moon's confidence came back.

Bart shut the door then got in the passenger side. Seat belt on, Moon stared out of the window at the passing scenery, the area dark. Blocks of flats. Houses. Wherever they were going, it wasn't into the hub of the city—bikes were prevalent there, and trams, and a fuck load of people. After a while, a hotel came up on the left, *his* hotel. It was a couple of miles away from the centre.

The driver turned into the slip road that curved round to the front of the hotel and stopped outside it. Grass surrounded the building, tall trees dotted here and there. A couple of smokers stood beneath a canopy of branches, taking no notice of the SUV. If this had been back in London, those smokers would be Moon's men, positioned to ensure nothing got out of hand.

"Henrik's men?" Moon asked.

Bart glanced over at them. "I do not know them." He got out, opening Moon's door.

Moon squinted up at him. "I thought I'd be killing whoever tonight. Why have you brought me here?"

"You are. Stop asking questions. Curiosity killed the cat."

Was that supposed to scare me?

Moon held back laughter.

Bart handed over a folded slip of paper and Moon's phone, his wallet, plus a second phone. "Follow the instructions. If I do not receive confirmation inside two hours, there will be trouble. My number is in this new phone. Only contact me on that. Stay here afterwards. Goodnight."

Moon left the car and slid the paper and phones in his trouser pocket, desperate to see what was on the note. Not giving Bart a chance to change his mind, he strolled into the hotel, the reception desk straight ahead. The woman behind it didn't bat an eyelid, which was odd. He hadn't been here for a while, had never seen her before, so why wasn't she questioning him, asking if he needed help?

Maybe she doesn't give a shit. It's late, she might not want to be here.

He walked to the right, past clusters of seating, stopping to take some complimentary teabag, coffee, and sugar sachets, some little portions of milk—he needed a brew. He stuffed them in his suit jacket pocket and veered left to the lifts. Mindful there might be cameras, he pressed the UP button and waited. Glanced to the wall of windows at the end of the seating area and caught sight of the SUV driving back down the curving road, the light from the streetlamps glinting off its roof, the men's shapes visible. He relaxed a little, although not enough to erase the tension brought on by the upcoming murder.

The lift arrived, and he stepped on. Chose the button for his floor. He ascended, keeping a poker face in case CCTV monitored him—if this went tits up and the police became involved, he had to appear innocent not shifty. At his room, he took the card from his wallet and used it to enter. Shut the door. Leaned on it to gather his thoughts.

This was madness.

Murder abroad. Sounded like a bad film title.

He sorted the lights and went straight for the kettle. It was empty—the room had been tidied in his absence—so he filled it in the bathroom and flicked it on.

He sat on the end of the bed, dreading reading the note now the time had come. He had less than two hours, but ten minutes of drinking tea and messaging Debbie wouldn't hurt. But Hendrik might have placed some kind of app on his mobile, so he'd have to be careful what he wrote.

Fuck, would he have seen I got hold of Debbie at the house, even though I deleted it?

Surely not, if Hendrik had sent him out to kill. Or was this a test to see if Moon would do it? Still, he'd watch himself, but he had a way to let her know all wasn't well, but to anyone reading, it would seem like everything was fine.

MOON: I'M BACK AT THE HOTEL. LITTLE MISUNDERSTANDING REGARDING BUSINESS. I'M OKAY WITH IT NOW SO SHOULD BE HOME SOON. GOT A BIT OF INDIGESTION, THOUGH.

He always suffered when stressed, and she knew that, he'd grumbled about it enough, that being a leader would kill him eventually. Would she get what he was saying?

DEBBIE: I WAS SO WORRIED YOU HAVE DOUBLE TROUBLE COMING YOUR WAY.

He smiled. She was savvy, his missus. A fucking diamond. The way she'd worded that, without a full stop after 'worried' — to anyone else it would read as an innocent sentence.

MOON: I'VE GOT A NEW VENTURE THEY WANT ME TO DO, SIMILAR TO YOURS, BUT THE GIRLS HAVE NO CHOICE.

DEBBIE: I CAN HELP YOU WITH IT BEFORE YOU GET BACK IF NEEDED.

She was telling him she'd get hold of the other leaders and see what she could do from London. Not a lot, but he appreciated her for trying.

MOON: I'LL BE OKAY.

DEBBIE: WHAT DO YOU HAVE TO SORT BEFORE YOU COME HOME?

MOON: NOTHING I CAN'T HANDLE, BUT GOD, MY BODY'S KILLING ME.

DEBBIE: [SHOCKED EMOJI] SERIOUSLY? IT'S THAT BAD? WILL IT POSE A PROBLEM?

MOON: I DON'T KNOW. I'D BETTER GO. GOT A LITTLE JOB TO DO NOW.

DEBBIE: OKAY, SPEAK SOON. LOVE YOU.

MOON: LOVE YOU, TOO.

She'd be fretting, but at least she could relate what he'd said to The Brothers, give them a heads-up that he had to murder someone. Had they managed to get a flight yet? Or had they opted for the Eurostar? All she'd said was double trouble was coming. She'd probably thought it best not to mention the time they'd arrive.

Moon made tea. Took the note out and read it.

GO TO THE ROOM TO THE LEFT OF YOURS.
INTRODUCE YOURSELF.
EXECUTE OUR ORDER.
TAKE PHOTOS OF YOU WITH THE RESULT.
SEND TO ME.
DISPOSE OF THE RUBBISH.

Moon frowned. How the fuck was he supposed to dispose of a body without being seen? He couldn't carry it out of the hotel. Maybe he should switch the process round. Get the occupant into Rembrandtpark, kill them, *then* dispose, perhaps in the pond? And which 'left' was the correct one? If he was standing in front of his door? Or if he was inside his room?

"Fuck's sake."

He checked the new phone for contacts. Only Bart's name. He'd have to send a message—he couldn't fuck this up by killing the wrong person in the wrong room. Or didn't it matter which side he killed? Did they just want any old body as proof he was trustworthy? Was the target an innocent holidaymaker?

MOON: WHICH LEFT?

BART: GO INTO THE CORRIDOR. FACE YOUR DOOR. THAT LEFT.

Moon drank his tea. He was in desperate need of a shower and a change of clothes. He'd sort that afterwards. By the time his cup was empty, he'd formed a plan. He wasn't going to kill anyone. He'd explain to the occupant what was going on and hope they listened to him.

He slid both phones and keycard into his pocket and left his room. Faced the door. Stepped to the left until he stood in front of the target's. Who was it? Had they done something to upset Hendrik? And if the occupant had been chosen for a specific reason, how did Hendrik know this person was in the hotel?

Because he's runs an area. Has men to find these things out.

Moon knocked.

The door opened only a few inches, enough for a woman to stare out at him. Her wide eyes showed her fear, then confusion that *he* stood there and not someone else. Was she expecting

Hendrik or Bart? Moon reckoned she was around twenty, her blonde hair lying over one shoulder, her pyjamas pink with snowmen all over them.

"Do you speak English?" he asked.

"Yes."

"Do you know Hendrik Alderliesten?"

"Yes."

"Did he bring you here?"

"Yes."

"You have to come with me." Moon thought about her luggage, a possible passport. The room being bugged. He whispered, "Go and get your passport and any important belongings—your money, a purse, whatever."

"I am going to England now?" she whispered back.

"Maybe. Got any makeup?"

She frowned. "Yes…"

"Bring that, too."

She closed the door, and he cursed himself for not sticking his foot in the gap to prevent that. But it opened again, and she emerged holding a large handbag, clothing piled on top. He held her wrist gently, leading her to his room. Once inside, and again thinking *his* room could have been bugged while he'd been in that backstreet house, he took her into the bathroom and shut the door.

Keeping his voice as low as possible, he said, "Do not scream or make a noise. It's important that you listen, understand?"

She nodded.

"I've been sent to kill you." He flashed his hand out to cover her gaping mouth. "No noise, remember. They could be listening." He paused, gave her a gentle smile to show he wasn't a threat. But the smile might not calm her. He was under no illusions he was an ugly, scary-looking bastard. "I'm not going to kill you, but I'll make out I did. The makeup…any blue eyeshadow? Purple?"

She bobbed her head.

"I'll put it on so it's like bruises on your neck. I have to take pictures, send them. You'll have to pretend you're dead on my bed, right?" He took his hand away.

"But he promised me good work in England."

"He lied." Moon thought about any bugs again. "Can I trust you to stay here while I book you another room?"

"If I leave, he will kill my brother, so I will stay."

That old chestnut. "Promise me you will."

"I will."

"And if you still want to go to England, you can come back with me when…when me and my friends have dealt with Hendrik."

"You will not kill my brother?"

"Fuck, no." He explained what Hendrik wanted him to do, being a pimp. "That's not my style, got it? If that's the work you want to do, fine, my girlfriend will sort you out, but I'm not a danger to you, I'm trying to bloody help you."

She nodded once again, her shoulders slumping. Relief?

He *had* to have faith in her, because there was no way he'd kill her unless he had to — unless she became a nuisance to him and it meant he couldn't go home.

Moon left the room and returned to reception.

Chapter Two

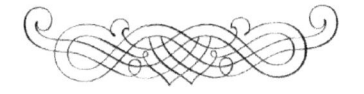

Ineke Meijer crept from the bathroom. Faint steam rose lazily from the kettle spout, and to stop herself from thinking too much about what that man had said—*murder?*—she clicked the switch and opened a coffee sachet. She made her drink and sat on the bed, trying to work out what to do. Was this a trick? To see if she ran? How could she when Christoffel's life would be in danger?

Her ten-year-old half-brother didn't deserve to be dragged into this. He lived a good and honest life with their father and his mamma, Greet. Ineke's mother wasn't in the picture anymore, thank God, and if she was, she wouldn't be much help here. Nor would her father, who'd left her with Moeder when she was two, only seeing her once a month for a few hours.

Ineke had never told him of the abuse she'd suffered, how Moeder was a bitch in a good woman's clothing—he'd assumed life had been a bed of roses for his daughter, and why would he think different? Moeder had shown him her good side whenever he'd arrived to pick Ineke up. He felt that any problems she had, she should work through them by herself. Something about building character and needing a backbone in this hard-faced world. Ineke had long since accepted that was his way of distancing himself from her and any troubles, and if she phoned him and explained this mess, he'd say, "You got yourself into it, so find a way out."

Even though he was a lawyer and should want to help.

He hated the fact she was a sex worker, even going so far as to say she couldn't see Christoffel, it would taint him, and she was an embarrassment, and why couldn't she have gone into business or nursing? That had been her plan, she'd enrolled in the University of Amsterdam, but with no one to pay her tuition fees, she'd had to work to fund her education. Her course had been full-time, so she'd rented a little glass-fronted room to offer her services at night. People staring at her when they weren't supposed to—foreigners who didn't know the rules about that, or they just didn't care. Going to the front door to discuss payment—one hundred euros to use her body. Relying on her gut instinct on whether to let a client inside. She had made a lot of money, enough to live well despite her fees, and it had become addictive.

If only she'd stayed home sick the night Hendrik had paid for her time. She hadn't been well, light-headed from tiredness, exhausted and on the verge of burnout. Her Asset Management course was demanding, taking a lot out of her, but she'd turned up to her job anyway, worried about losing it if she didn't.

His promise of her working and earning as a high-class escort in England had given her a new lease of life, hope spreading. And she should have known not to have hope. He was going to run a sex business in secret, using a man in London to oversee everything. He'd paid off her remaining tuition fees for the year so there was nothing outstanding when she dropped her course. She'd have to give it back out of her wages—and he said she could finish her studies in the UK. So why had she been sequestered in this hotel for so long, only ever seeing that horrible Bart and the room service people when they'd brought her food? Had he been waiting for the London man to take her on a plane?

It had all seemed so perfect.

"When things seem too good to be true, they usually are."

Moeder had regularly said that, and in this instance it turned out she was right. Once Ineke had been brought to the hotel, Hendrik had told her the real terms of the agreement, and if she didn't obey, he'd kill Christoffel. He knew where he lived, where he went to school, and what clubs he attended—football and chess, the former to teach him he could be a star on the field if he tried hard enough, the latter to learn strategy, something their father had insisted on in case the football career didn't work out. A man who understood chess would go far if coupled with the right business path. The poor boy had high expectations sitting on his shoulders.

Hendrik had gripped her face, his other hand around her throat, and made it clear she had no choice. And she believed him. She hadn't tried to escape. Hendrik had frightened her so much she hadn't dared—he was like Monster from her past, someone she obeyed without question. And that Bart man, he'd come to check on her, taking what he wanted without payment, a knife to the throbbing pulse in her neck. He'd produced photos of Christoffel, the times when he was alone, showing her what an easy target her brother was. Christoffel walked back from football on his own. He took a tram to and from chess. Such a little boy for his age, no match for wiry men, or Bart and Hendrik who were bigger. He wouldn't be able to get away if they snatched him.

She sipped her black coffee and thought of the other man. The bald one sent to kill her. Wasn't he afraid of Hendrik? Was he brave enough to only pretend to kill her? What if Hendrik wanted to see her body in person? What then? Whoever the newcomer was, he had something about him that spoke of authority, a man not to cross, yet at the same time seemed genuine. Did he have a daughter and that was why he was helping her? Did Ineke remind him of her? Or was it a granddaughter? He was old enough to have one. He'd said he had a girlfriend who could help her. Was that a ploy to get her to believe him? Was *he* the London man who'd be in charge of the sex workers? Was the girlfriend the woman who'd keep everyone in line?

Ineke had read about trafficking, it was hard not to, what with it being in the news, but she'd never thought she'd be involved. Never thought she'd be taken out of Amsterdam, where sex work was legal, to a place where it wasn't. Surely Hendrik could have just ordered her to pay him some of her wages here. If money was what he wanted, that would have been so simple.

There's probably more money in it for him in the UK. He said I'd be an escort. Don't they charge thousands a night?

And another thing. Why had he allowed her to keep her passport, her purse, only taking her phone away? It didn't make sense. She could buy a ticket and fly out of here. But he might have someone hidden in the outskirts close to the hotel, waiting with a gun to take her down should she leave the building.

And there's Christoffel. I can't let them kill him.

The door clicked, and she almost dropped her coffee in fright. The bald man walked in, and she placed the cup on the desk. Stood. He beckoned to her to come forward, then gestured to her bag which she'd left on the bed. A finger to his lips, he turned and walked out, holding the door open for her.

"Shh," he said and led her towards the lift.

They stepped in, Ineke's heart seeming to clank around, missing beats then thudding hard with the rush of adrenaline. They ascended one floor, and he guided her to another room. Inside, he let out a sigh of relief.

"Thank fuck for that." He walked to the bedroom area. "We need to talk. You can unpack your bag. We haven't got long. I was given a timeframe."

She sat on a chair in the corner by the window, clutching her handbag to her belly and taking things out to place them on the desk next to her.

He paced and told her everything he'd experienced since coming to Amsterdam. He'd been kept in a room in that backstreet house, the one she'd hated and got bad vibes from. She'd met Hendrik there the day after his proposition to finalise the plans. Then he'd taken her to the hotel.

"Why did you return after the first time if you did not want to do what he said?" she asked, confused. Did he suffer like she did, where if he was given orders, he obeyed? She was trying not to do that so often; she had to remind herself she was free from her past and didn't have to answer to anyone, but a lifetime of being indoctrinated meant she slipped into her old ways from time to time. She hadn't been in *that* life for two years, but trying to erase the eighteen previous to that from her memory, her psyche, was proving harder than she'd imagined.

"Fuck knows. He wanted to apologise in person, something he's apparently known for. And to be honest, because I'm selfish. I had a good time before, wanted the same again. Yet I've got a woman at home waiting for me. I could have taken her somewhere on holiday if I wanted a laugh or whatever, but instead I chose to come back here. I'm a bastard and need to make it up to her. I only thought about myself. Still, if this has taught me a lesson, it's that Debbie should be the most important thing to me, along with my Estate, not getting high in the Netherlands."

"Debbie is your girlfriend?"

"Yeah."

"Did she know what Hendrik wanted you to do for him in London?"

"Not then, but she has an idea now." He told her about Debbie's business and sat on the bed as if tired. "So if that's what you want to do, she can set you up. It's all got to be kept quiet, obviously, because you can't solicit in the UK, but... Do you even *want* to live in London?"

"Since Hendrik mentioned it, I have wanted to go there. A new life, something I have wanted since I was a little girl." She paused, recalling how often she'd dreamed of flying off. "Away from here. The memories. But will Hendrik hurt my brother anyway once I am 'dead'?"

"I'm hoping he won't have the chance. There's these two men, see... They're called The Brothers, twins, and they run another Estate. Let me explain some of that so you understand what London's like."

She listened, astounded that these men, and even women, could rule sections of the city and the police didn't seem to do anything about it. Then again, should she have been shocked? It was clear Hendrik did a similar thing, although she'd never heard about him until the night he'd stared at her through her red-light window. Yet in London, it seemed everyone knew who looked after which Estate, and they welcomed it, even — or maybe that was this man's perception, that they had all the residents in hand. It had strands of her past in it, where people were manipulated, told what to do, how to behave. Maybe London was the best place for her. She functioned better with order, knowing the rules.

"What is your name?" she asked.

"Moon."

"That is weird."

He chuckled and got up to open the window. Took a slim complimentary cigar from the desk and lit it.

"The smoke alarm will go off," she warned him. How could he be so silly as to draw attention to this room? Hendrik's men could be watching. If the alarm sounded, they'd have to go outside. Or was that what Moon was doing? Intentionally finding a seemingly innocent way to get her out of this room so he *could* kill her? God, she didn't know whether to trust him or not. Monster had ruined any chance she had of fully allowing herself to believe someone.

He stuck the cigar outside, still holding it, and sucked on it through the gap. "I'll risk it."

"It says on the information sheet they will ask you to leave if you do that. Where will we go then? What if Hendrik's men grab me when we go outside?"

"All right, bloody hell." Moon stubbed the cigar out on the glass. He tossed it on the desk and wafted his arms around, shepherding the smoke towards the window. "Spray some of that deodorant, for fuck's sake."

Ineke reached over for her dark-blue can and pumped the nozzle. She flapped her hands to disperse the scent. "What happens now?"

"First, we stage the murder. Then you'll stay here until it's all over. I'll go out in the morning to buy you some food. We can't risk the room service people recognising you—I assume that's how you've been fed."

"Yes. What does 'it's all over' mean?"

He flumped onto the bed. "When Hendrik and his men are killed. How many did you meet?"

"There were six of them in the house at Slotervaart and a dirty-looking man who drove me here. I was taken to a room with a table and chairs in it."

"I know the one. I only saw six in total an' all, plus that driver, so maybe that's his whole crew. A small outfit, then. Shouldn't be problem to get to the lot of them, although the driver might be tricky. But maybe he's no one to worry about. The Brothers will no doubt have some plan or other for that, or I'll have to come up with one. Tell me what I need to know about the police here, what to look out for, where to dump bodies."

She told him everything—or what she could think of anyway—and finished with, "Rembrandtpark might be a good place to leave their bodies. It could seem like a serial killer on the loose or something." Had that sounded ridiculous? "You know what I mean."

"Yeah. It's a pisser not knowing the layout of this city. In London, I'd know exactly where to go and what to do."

"What about getting them to come here, to my other room? Hendrik must have paid for it using one of his cards—even with cash, it could be linked back to him by CCTV or the phone if he booked that way, so if the police know who he is, they might put it down to a business deal gone wrong."

"But your fingerprints are in there, DNA or whatever. No, it's best not to do it here. We could murder them in that house. Just leave them inside." He nodded. "Yeah, that'd work. Okay, let's get cracking." His phoned bleeped. "Hang on." He read a message and smiled. "The twins' flight's at eight in the morning, so we'll just have to hang tight until they arrive."

"Okay."

"Do you have a phone?"

"Hendrik took it."

"Did he nab your passport as well?"

"No."

Moon narrowed his eyes. "That's fucking odd, that is. Did he frighten you so much that you wouldn't run?"

She nodded.

Moon sighed. "Is there any family you want to contact once Hendrik and his lot have been killed? You mentioned a brother, so…"

"Christoffel is ten. My mother...I don't have to worry about her, and my father would just tell me to not involve him. He doesn't like...being a part of my life."

"Tosser."

"What is that?"

"A bastard."

"Ah, yes, he is one of those, although it took me years to realise it. So no, I will not contact anyone, and if I do, I will wait until I get to London. I know their numbers, they are in my head."

"I'll sort you with a new phone, somewhere to live. Saying that, The Brothers will likely be the ones to rent a flat to you—they've got a few, they're always buying the bloody things—and if you're going to work for Debbie, you're better off on Cardigan."

"Their Estate?"

"Yeah. Right, let's get this makeup sorted, then I'll take the pictures."

Ineke thought for a moment about how *bizarre* this was to have someone accept this scenario as if it were normal. Perhaps for him it was. She'd been through such a lot in her childhood that this was normal to her, too; she'd accepted awful things and lived as best she could in the circumstances, the same as she was now. If she thought too deeply about it, it was frightening how her mind had been manipulated and she just did as she was told. Could she get help with that? Train herself to be the opposite?

She trusted Moon, even if she shouldn't and would regret it later, and unless he was a good actor, she believed he was on her side.

"I'll get a cheap phone for you before we leave, actually," he said. "You can speak to Debbie and decide if this is what you want to do. Once Hendrik isn't a threat, there's no reason why you can't stay in Amsterdam if you want."

She could, but she didn't want to. What was left for her here except a little brother she rarely saw? Although their father had never been enamoured with her, he treated Christoffel differently, like a prince, so he'd be okay. She didn't need to remain in case he needed her.

"No, London," she said firmly. "I want a brand-new life."

Chapter Three

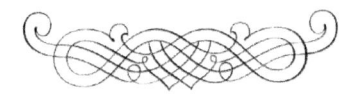

Monster stood in the bathroom, hands on hips, slender fingers splayed over her expensive dress, red fabric to match her nails and lips. She smelled of spicy perfume, freshly sprayed. Her hair, styled by the lady from the salon who'd just left, was so nice. Shiny. A blonder tint to it. Monster would be going out tonight, then. On the prowl for those men

she liked to bring home. The ones she sent away before Ineke got out of bed in the morning.

Monster tapped her foot. "Moeder says lick the floor."

Ineke got down on her hands and knees. The cleaner had been today, so the floor wasn't dirty, but still, she hated doing this. Licking the droplets from where her mother had stood on the tiles and dried herself after her shower. Ineke always had to use a mat, but not Moeder. She was exempt from that rule and many others.

Moeder was awful when she was in this sort of mood, her day ruined by the people she dealt with. She took it out on Ineke—her little slave as she liked to privately call her. Ineke wished she could tell someone, but who'd believe her?

No one.

She was just a child, Moeder telling people she was prone to exaggeration and making up stories, whereas Moeder was a pillar of society, that's what she'd said. Someone people looked up to. Or hated, depending on who they were. As a judge, she was respected, sometimes putting people in prison for doing exactly what she did to Ineke. She was proud of getting away with it, she crowed about it when she became Monster. Words slurring from alcohol, she spoke about the parents she'd had in her court, how their children had blabbed about their treatment, and look where they were now! In care homes with other brats who didn't know how to keep their mouths shut.

If you opened it, bad things happened. You were raped—Ineke didn't know what that was. Slapped. Locked in a cupboard with no food. Chained to radiators, your back burning from the heat. You became niemand. Nobody. But wasn't Ineke niemand anyway? Wasn't she just existing the best way she knew how until she could get out of here? When she was old enough, she'd leave, but even at her age now she worried she wouldn't be able to. Wouldn't have the courage.

She licked up each droplet of water, Monster's damp footprints, knowing what would come next. So she took her time to hold off the inevitable, also knowing what would happen if she took a little too *long. She had to time it just right or she might get kicked.*

"There, such a good little slave. Get up."

Ineke rose. She didn't look at Monster. She didn't want to see her pretty face. Most times she stared at her hairline with its golden strands that draped over one side of her forehead in a giant curl. Perfect, she was, so delicate and beautiful, yet to Ineke she was the ugliest person she'd ever seen when she was Monster.

Even though he wasn't much help, Ineke longed for Vader to come, to take her away and never bring her back, but her father didn't see her that often, preferring his life without her in it—neither parent cared whether they hurt her feelings with the things they said. Ineke supposed she should never have been born; they didn't want her, and she didn't want them. She was the reason why they'd divorced.

But even though Monster was cruel, Ineke was safe despite the abuse—safe because it was all she'd known, and it was better to stay where you knew the rules than go somewhere else and not know any. Where there were dark cupboards and starvation. Yet at the same time she'd love to fly away, to another country, far from Moeder and her drinking bouts, her weird and confusing personalities. But she'd miss baby Christoffel, who grew more and more each time she saw pictures of him. He was her reason for living now.

"You've got spit on the floor," Monster said. "Dirty girl. Disgusting, hideous, filthy girl. Mop it."

Ineke left the bathroom and walked downstairs to the cleaning cupboard. Monster followed, her delicate feet padding on the white carpet. Ineke reached inside to pull out the mop, still damp from the cleaning lady using it, and picked up the bucket. She filled it at the kitchen sink, Monster's hot breath on the top of her head where she stood so close. A squirt of washing-up liquid produced a dome of bubbles. She shut the tap off and carried the mop and bucket upstairs.

She washed the floor, Monster in the doorway, leaning on the jamb, arms folded. Ineke zoned out the fact she was being watched, used to it. Job almost finished, she paused for her senses to pick up that Monster had stepped away onto the landing. Ineke continued mopping to the threshold, then waited for her next instruction.

"Pour the water in the toilet."

Ineke held back a sigh. This game, it was so predictable now.

So she didn't slip — Monster would laugh at that — she carefully tiptoed over the wet floor and raised the bucket.

"You've made footprints. Mop again."

This went on twice more, then Monster got tired of playing.

"Empty it in the downstairs toilet."

Ineke obeyed, putting the things away afterwards. Monster sat at the kitchen island on a stool, watching Ineke who stood at the cleaning cupboard door. How could someone who looked like a Barbie be so nasty?

"You may microwave your food."

Ineke took the meal from the fridge. Moeder paid a lady to cook for them, they received a once-a-week delivery. Each of the plastic containers had a sticker on top with instructions for each day. Every week, the same meals on the same days.

Monster liked control. Order.

Ineke popped the food in the microwave for the time stated on the label.

"You will eat from the container. Get a knife and fork out."

Ineke obeyed again, fulfilling the other instructions: put a placemat down; pour a glass of water; butter a slice of bread; take a yoghurt and spoon out for after dinner—"Strawberry, it has to be strawberry for a Friday, so why have you picked cherry, you stupid child?"

Once Ineke had settled at the island, Monster left her alone. She'd probably gone to get her drink from the living room. At last, Ineke could breathe easier, although she was still on edge in case Monster came back in with another order. Then there was the worry of Dorothea coming, the old lady who lived in Slotervaart and cycled over. She'd been naughty once, Moeder sending her to prison for two years, and now Dorothea babysat for free to repay her for the light sentence. Two years instead of five was a good deal.

Dorothea didn't like babysitting and made sure Ineke knew it.

Meal finished, she rinsed her things and stacked them in the dishwasher. Without being told, she took her schoolbag from a cupboard and got on with her homework. Moeder said she must study, become someone important like her, not an embarrassment. Vader said the same. The pressure to do well was a driving force, something to concentrate on rather than what she went through. When she read books, she sometimes forgot everything but what the words on the page showed her—beaches, magical lands, fairies who lived inside flower petals. But then real life intruded, reminding her she hadn't escaped into another world, the realisation bringing on tears.

What had they been like as a couple? Ineke could only remember living with Moeder. Her time with Vader here was a complete mystery, but she'd imagined it often enough: Moeder ordering him around, him doing the same to her until they'd clashed so much he'd walked out and never came back. Had she been Monster with him, too? Or had the drinking started after he'd gone?

Her mother had boyfriends. She brought them home after her nights out, young men who'd been in her court for doing bad things, selected so she could control them. Secret, they had to be a secret. No one outside the house must know what she did in her bedroom and who with. Monster, still drunk, told her all about it the next morning over breakfast. The things they did — rude things.

The doorbell chimed, and Ineke sighed. Dorothea was here, and it would be a different type of control now, right up until nine o'clock when she had to go to bed. The woman trundled into the kitchen with her backpack, slinging it on the floor, the front door slamming as Monster left without saying goodbye.

She never did.

"Take that and get it sorted," Dorothea snapped, pointing to her backpack. She stripped off her clothes and dumped them on the bag.

Ineke ignored the nakedness, she'd seen it too often to be shocked. She put her homework away, picked up the bitch's stuff, and went into the utility room. She stared at the clothes, disgusted by the knickers, the filthy socks. She put them in the washing machine, then emptied the bag in there. Set it on a short cycle so it would dry in time before Monster got back.

Dorothea would have locked the front door and be in the shower by now. While she waited, Ineke sat at the island, thinking about getting on a plane and flying away. Dorothea called to her, so she walked upstairs, finding the woman exactly where she always was on nights like this—sitting at Moeder's vanity table, only a towel covering her body. Her brush that she always kept in her coat pocket lay on her lap.

Ineke dried and styled Dorothea's hair—Monster would be so drunk when she got back that she wouldn't even notice the change in the woman. The scalp was flaky, some sore spots with scabs. If Monster ever found out about this, Ineke would pay for not telling her, for keeping secrets. But what else could she to do? As punishment for Ineke not obeying her, Dorothea was good at saying she'd been naughty while she looked after her, resulting in Monster storming into her bedroom, waking her up, and slapping the backs of her legs once the old cow had gone home.

Hair dried, Dorothea turned around and stuck her foot out. Ineke selected some polish and clippers then knelt. She hated this part; Dorothea's toes had built-up skin around the nails and black gunk beneath the ends. Ineke cut the nails, scraped at the rough skin and dirt, then painted over the previous polish from last week. How did her toes get in such a mess in seven days?

"I need a trim." Dorothea stood and whipped the towel off.

Ineke swallowed. Stretched to put the polish and clippers away. She used Moeder's small scissors from a drawer and snipped the hairs covering Dorothea's private parts, hot tears stinging. Disgusting job over, she took the towel and left Dorothea to put on one of Moeder's dressing gowns while she waited for her clothes to be ready. Ineke hung the towel up and cleaned the shower. Collected the hoover to get rid of the hairs, the nails, the dirt, then sat in her room until Dorothea shouted for her to come and fold the dry washing.

It was strange, this, how Ineke just did as she was told. She knew it was wrong, somewhere in her manipulated mind. Little voices sometimes urged her to tell Vadar, or a teacher, or a random stranger on the street, but she never did.

She was too afraid to.

Because of the bad things that could happen.

Chapter Four

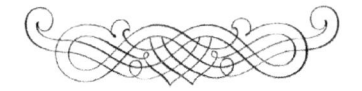

Moon stared at the woman. He didn't even know her name, which, now he came to think of it, was bloody odd of him not to have asked. He cleared his throat. "Err, what do I call you?"

She lay on the bed, posed in her pyjamas as if dead. Legs bent, pointing to one side. Hands up either side of her face. So still. Disturbing.

Another odd thing, because dead bodies didn't usually bother him, they were just something to get rid of afterwards, yet this whole scenario was off as fuck, unnerving him. Maybe because he wasn't in full control, Hendrik tugging some of his strings. He'd likely feel better once the twins arrived. Reinforcements to remind him of who he was and what he was capable of.

She didn't move a muscle. "Ineke."

"This isn't quite right. Excuse me a second." He didn't normally sound apologetic for anything he was doing, but he needed to act calm, he didn't want to spook her. He fished in her makeup bag and took out a red lipstick and a slim brush, one like Debbie used to line her mouth before she filled it in with colour. "I've strangled a fair few people, so I know what they look like when they've snuffed it, and something's missing."

"You've *what*?"

Me and my big mouth. "I'll go into more detail about what a leader does later, but for now, trust me. I've said I'm not going to kill you and I won't. I've just got to adjust your makeup a bit, all right?"

He knelt on the bed, bent over her, and slid the skinny bristles over the lipstick. He dotted it around her eyes, eyelids, and the tops of her cheeks to create the spots that would normally be present after a throttling, then checked the whites—they were already marked with the lightning strikes of scarlet veins, so that was good. As well as the blue and purple 'bruises' they'd created between them, on her neck in the shape of a thumb and finger marks, he reckoned she'd pass. *If* they didn't look too closely. That lipstick job seemed obvious that it was fake to him, but maybe that's because he knew it was.

He got off, tossing the brush and lipstick into her bag. "Right, hold your breath and stare at the ceiling." Phone out, he snapped an image or two, then returned to the bed to lie beside her.

She stiffened but retained her pose, asking warily, "What are you doing?"

"This is fucking weird, but they want me in a picture. Insurance. Sorry, I should have warned you I was getting on the bed beforehand. I'm not used to taking people's feelings into consideration, I just do what I want." He took two more photos and sat up to check what they looked like. "They'll do." He sent them to Bart with a message.

MOON: WILL DISPOSE OF THE RUBBISH NOW.

BART: NICE CHOICE OF METHOD. NO BLOOD.

MOON: THOUGHT THAT WAS BEST.

BART: WHERE ARE YOU TAKING HER?

MOON: THERE'S AN UNDERGROUND CAR PARK HERE.

BART: SHE WILL BE FOUND BY MORNING. GOOD.

He showed Ineke the string of texts for full transparency. It was better that he was open with her every step of the way so she trusted him more.

"Why is it good I will be found so quickly?" she asked.

"I don't know." Realisation hit him hard. "D'you know what, I think they're playing me. They don't want me to work for them at all. They're teaching me a lesson for refusing. This is a fucking setup. I reckon they always meant to kill you and just used me to do it."

She laughed, although it came out unsteady, as if she couldn't get over how frightening this all was. Maybe it was her way of processing what he'd said. "If they send those images to the police, they will look stupid when you bring them to this room and I am alive. We could say we were just messing about with the makeup. Would that work?"

There was some sense of amusement in that, seeing the coppers' faces, proving Hendrik wrong, but… "We can't have Hendrik knowing you're not dead. Christoffel…"

She sat up, her smile gone. "Then what do we do?"

"I'll think of something."

Moon ferreted in her handbag in case she was lying about not having her phone, but there wasn't one. He found it weird that Ineke didn't ask why he felt he could just rummage around in there without permission. She accepted it as though her needs didn't matter. Either she felt it was best to let him do whatever he wanted or there was some other reason why it appeared she didn't think she had a choice. Hadn't he settled her nerves enough by saying he wouldn't kill her?

"Listen, I swear to God, I'm not going to hurt you. I know it's hard to believe, but we're going to sort this, okay?"

"Okay."

He tried to think of a way to alleviate her fears about her brother. If she didn't have him to worry about, she'd be more likely to trust him. "Look, would your father listen if I told him he needs to take Christoffel and his wife away somewhere for a while?"

"No. He'd phone the police." Ineke shook her head as though dislodging the images inside it.

"What's the matter? You've gone all pale."

"I am scared because I do not know all the rules or what is going to happen." Her bottom lip trembled. "I do not expect you to understand, but I have struggled with life since I left home. I had to create my own order so I could cope."

Her own order? What did that mean? Seeing as she was having a bit of a wobble, he wasn't going to tell her *he* was scared, too. A bit. Doing this crap in a foreign country could bring all sorts of hassle to his door, and he was uneasy to say the least. "It'll be all right, I'll fix everything. Go and wash your face and neck."

She wandered to the bathroom and closed the door. Moon thought about how he'd phrase the next stage of his plan to Bart. Sitting here for about an hour should make it seem plausible.

Ineke returned, her face red and shiny, and Moon made them coffee. He opened up, telling her his role on The Moon Estate, about how he'd killed people, his life before Debbie, how it had changed so much since he'd met her.

"You love her," Ineke said.

"I do, and I need to show it more. Coming here again was a mistake."

"A big one."

"You're not wrong. I'm angry they've brought you into this. Using you as a way to make a point. Like your life doesn't matter so long as Hendrik makes me see he's in charge."

"My life has never mattered. What I want or need has not come into the equation."

"That doesn't sound good."

"No. But I am trying to change my mindset, so we could look at it a different way. Life supposedly takes you where you need to go so certain things can happen—those things shape you, make you into who you are. Everyone involved has to be at the same place at the same time. I wanted a better life, and now I can have it. Maybe the universe or fate has decided I do not need any more shit. Maybe you were sent here to make sure that happens."

"God, are you into all that mumbo-jumbo destiny bollocks?"

She shrugged. "It is better to think that than see my life up until now for what it really was—I did not have it easy."

"True." *Has she learned a coping mechanism? What the fuck happened to her before all this?* "Tell me about you. Who's Ineke?"

She chuffed out a laugh. "I do not even know who I am. Perhaps I will finally find out in London. But if you want to know my story... Are you used to hearing about childhood abuse?"

"Yep."

"It is not pretty."

"I don't expect it is. Your father?"

"No, never him."

"Who, then?"

"The one person who is never supposed to hurt you." She smiled sadly. "My mother."

Ineke's tale had stabbed Moon in the heart. He was generally a hard bastard, shutting off his emotions, but this? He knew this kind of shit happened, but how this young woman was still standing, with all her marbles, he didn't know. "Jesus fucking Christ. Why didn't you tell anyone?"

"No one would believe me."

"Because of who she is."

"Yes."

"Where is she now?"

"That is a story for another day."

"Ah." Maybe that was her way of saying she couldn't face talking about it anymore. He wanted to give her some hope, something to latch on to. "The twins will like you. They've got a soft spot for people who've had it tough. You watch, they'll set you up in London and look after you. I've got to warn you, though, they're massive, they seem scary, and George can be a bit…direct, and he barks a lot. Comes off as an arsehole sometimes. But truth be told, he's the softer one of the two deep down. But however you feel when you meet them, just know they're your ticket to a better life. And I am. Debbie, too. We're all involved in what to some would seem like bad shit, gangsters running around and whatnot, but there are no better people to have in your corner."

She nodded. He wanted to convince her more, but that might come across as overegging the pudding. His actions would speak louder, and him not killing her, instead keeping her safe in a new room, had likely gone a long way to settling her fears already. Although…she could be thinking he was tricking her, playing a game with Hendrik. She had that air about her where she was calculating what he said to see if she could detect an signs of duplicity. No wonder, considering what her so-called mother had put her through.

"Never open this door unless it's me or someone I've said it's okay to let in." He accessed his message app again. "I suppose I'd better do my best to sort this so the police aren't called." He held the burner phone so she could see it as he typed.

MOON: I PUT HER IN THE UNDERGROUND CAR PARK AT MY HOTEL. WAITED FOR A WHILE TO MAKE SURE I WASN'T SEEN. SOMEONE CAME AND TOOK THE BODY. WAS THAT YOU LOT?

BART: WHAT? NO!

MOON: THEN WE HAVE A PROBLEM.

BART: STAY PUT UNTIL I GET BACK TO YOU.

Ineke raised her eyebrows. "That will get them looking all over Amsterdam."

"And off our backs. I'd better go to my room in case Hendrik comes—or sends one of his men." He glanced at the desk where the information sheet lay, and rather than take liberties and poke in her handbag again, he said, "There's a pen in your bag. Can you get it out?"

She did that and handed it over.

Moon stood and scribbled down his, Debbie's, and the twins' numbers. "If you don't hear from me by eleven tomorrow morning, use that phone to ring me." He pointed to the one on the desk. "If I don't answer, it means I can't, so try this one instead." He jabbed a meaty fingertip at the twins' work burner number. "They'll be in Amsterdam by then. One is called George, the other is Greg. If that fails, get hold of Debbie. She'll arrange a flight for you. The safe word if *they* end up coming to get you is…" He tried to think of an appropriate word.

"Rijzen," she said.

"What's that mean?"

"Rise."

"Err, okay…?"

"Because that is what I am going to do. Rise to the top, stop being that person at the bottom of the heap. I am so sick of being down there."

He nodded. Admired her faith in getting a better life for herself. "Well, I'll be off, then. If shit hits the fan and I can warn you, I'll knock on your door. I know it'll be hard, but try and get some sleep."

He left her there and made his way to his room. Stripped ready for a shower. The burner bleeped, and he checked the screen.

BART: CAR AND DRIVER LOCATED. NO BODY. DRIVER WILL BE DEALT WITH.

Moon supposed they had someone in the police able to give them that information via CCTV footage, but that had happened pretty bloody quickly. Would that person become a problem?

MOON: OKAY.

BART: I WILL PICK YOU UP TOMORROW SO YOU CAN VIEW THE WOMEN AND SELECT WHO YOU WANT TO TAKE.

MOON: [THUMBS-UP EMOJI]

BART: BE READY AT ONE.

That would give him time to nip down the road to buy Ineke some food in the morning. He'd noted a long line of people outside a bakery on his previous visit. It had reminded him of the good old days, when people still queued for their bread. The tradition had remained here. But it was a fair old way down the road, so he'd take it slow. Exercise wasn't his best friend.

He got dressed and nipped back to Ineke's room and, because of the late hour, tapped on the door quietly.

"Safe word," she said from behind the wood.

"Rijzen."

She opened it wide, and he stepped inside to explain what was going on.

"At least this way I'll know where they're keeping all the girls," he said. "We can release them once the men are taken out."

"If they are elsewhere, then why did he bring me here? This is an expensive hotel."

"Maybe you weren't destined for the UK all along. Like I said before, maybe he always meant for you to be murdered."

She shivered. "Why, though? I do not understand."

"Me neither. Sleep," he said. "I'll be by in the morning with some grub."

"Grub?"

"Food."

He left her, once again returning to his room, hoping no one working here was in Hendrik's pocket. If they were, he'd know Moon had booked another room.

Shit. Didn't think of that one, did you, dickhead?

Chapter Five

Moeder was someone else this morning. No wine had passed her lips at breakfast. No vodka drunk straight from the bottle. As Monster, she was wicked, the worst she could be, but as Moeder she could still be cruel. The woman had many personalities, and Ineke had learned the signals for when each one would show up. Today, it was the kind version, the one who was sorry for everything she'd done—Lief/Lovely.

During these times, Ineke used to lap up the love like the water on the bathroom floor, letting herself drown in the apologies, the tender strokes to her head, the cuddles. But as she'd grown, she'd cottoned on that Lief didn't stick around for long.

Lief knew what she'd done was bad. Lief wanted to make everything better. She cooked instead of using the food in the containers. She cleaned the bathroom floor herself. They watched films together with popcorn and chocolate, and Lief laughed at the funny bits. She looked younger in the brief pockets of heaven on those days, a vision of hope for Ineke that this *time, Moeder would get stuck in her personality cycle and be Lief forever. But it only lasted a few seconds, that hope. It was silly to let it grow inside her, so she stubbed it out as violently as Dorothea put out her cigarettes on the path in front of the house whenever she went outside to smoke.*

Hope was dangerous.

Lief swirled around the living room to the music, her floaty, flower-print summer dress bloating with her movements. Ineke watched from the sofa, wanting to get up and join her, but Lief could disappear, and someone else would take her place. So she remained where she was, waiting for the emergence of Nors/Grumpy, who took over her mother in an instant, a switch being flicked. Or Verdrietig/Sad, who mourned the life she didn't have—one without Ineke in it, where she'd never have met Vader and fallen for his charms. She'd be a single woman, no responsibilities other than work. Verdrietig cried a lot and wished she was dead. That *person was the hardest to handle when she ran around the house clutching a bottle of pills.*

But Lief was here, for however long, so while Ineke relaxed a fraction, she didn't completely trust. The music changed to something slower, and Lief's face softened. She danced as though in a dream, her hands out by her sides, her hair swaying. Was this who Vader had met? Ineke could see why he'd married her if this was what he'd got. He'd once said it had all changed after Ineke was born, then medication came into it, depression. All Ineke's fault, because if Moeder hadn't become pregnant, she would have been Lief forever.

"Did you have fun at school today?" Lief asked.

"Yes." Although Ineke had been bullied by the new girl, she wouldn't say. Lief would go there and sort it out nicely, but Monster, Nors, or Verdrietig would make it worse.

"Your father will be here soon."

That would be why Moeder was Lief. She had to maintain that she was a good mother, the best. She sometimes touched Vader's arm and smiled up at him, especially since Christoffel had been born, saying they should try again, Vader moving back in, and she'd even look after the boy at weekends when he came to stay. Vader always said no, that he loved his new wife, and one stretch of time with Moeder was enough to put him off her for life. Despite those cutting words, Lief had remained in play, her smile frozen, although Ineke would have bet she'd needed a drink and wanted to become Monster, to rail at him, call him names, and hurt him. Instead, she'd waited until he'd dropped Ineke home, then out came the bottle. The mean words. The orders. The eventual slap, the strike so hard Ineke knew Monster thought she was hitting Vader.

Was this dancing, the happy Lief, forced? Did she have to make *herself be like this whenever Vader came to collect Ineke? That was the same as Ineke having to pretend she had a good life and was happy—it had become easy to fake it. And why would Moeder want him back if he didn't want her? Weren't her boyfriends enough? Or did she only want Vader because he was content elsewhere?*

The doorbell chimed, and Lief wafted off to answer it, a giggle floating behind her, likely so Vader thought she was laughing at something Ineke had said. It was all orchestrated, a movie she'd written herself, only most of the time, Vader didn't read the lines she'd written for him and the scenes didn't go as planned.

Ineke remained on the sofa, uneasy now she'd be faced with both parents, their dynamics. Squirming uncoiled in her belly, the worms she imagined were in there, and she lifted a hand ready to bite her nails. But she stopped herself. There could be no outward signs of anxiety. No one was allowed to see the evidence of what all sides of Moeder did to her or made her feel. Ragged nails, bruises where they shouldn't be, and saying you had a stomachache were off the list. Ineke had to smile as much as she could at school, be the model child.

It tired her out.

"Oh, you've brought the little one," Lief trilled. "How precious! Come in."

"Is she ready?"

"Of course. Darling, your father's here."

Ineke stood and walked into the foyer. She smiled at Christoffel in Vader's arms and took her shoes out of the cupboard, put them on, and stood beside Lief.

Christoffel stretched his arms out towards her, and Vader struggled to hold him still.

"Let's go." Vader strode to his car.

"Be good," Lief whispered, a glint of Nors in her eyes. "The best you can be, then he might come home. If he doesn't, it'll be your fault. Remember, I'm

counting on you to make him want to be with me. It's your job to make sure that happens."

Ineke didn't want that job, it was too much, but she nodded and stepped into the Saturday sunshine, glad Lief was behind her so she couldn't see the tears forming. Ineke was always good with Vader, but he never came home, so what else was she supposed to do?

Still, for now, Ineke had a few hours where she didn't have to think about it. And today wouldn't be filled with awkward silences because Christoffel was here. She got into the back of the car, Vader strapping her brother into his special seat.

Christoffel clapped in excitement. He barely knew her, yet he acted as if they saw each other all the time. Was that what babies were like? They saw another child and were instantly happy? Ineke wanted to believe he loved her, because no one else did, and it was nice to have someone who cared whether she was there or not.

Vader got in the driver's seat and drove away. "Have you been good?"

"Yes."

"How has your mamma been?"

"Fine."

"Does she go out on Friday nights?"

"Sometimes." Every Friday.

"I heard she has a boyfriend."

"No."

"I wish she did, she'd leave me alone, then," he muttered.

Ineke didn't think she was supposed to have heard that. *"She's waiting for you to come home."*

"Neuken."

That was a naughty word.

"Sorry, I shouldn't have said that." *Vader glanced at her in the rearview mirror and sighed.* *"I'm going to have to tell you. I'm never coming home. Your mamma and I...it wouldn't be right. I don't want you getting your hopes up."*

"I haven't. I won't."

"Good."

They weren't on the route to the bowling alley, so she asked, *"Where are we going?"*

"To my house. My wife wants to meet you."

Greet. Ineke had heard a lot about her from Monster, who said she was ugly and fat, a pig.

"Don't tell your mamma," he said. *"As far as she's concerned, we went for lunch and bowled as usual."*

The idea of keeping a secret excited Ineke at first, something that belonged to just her, Vader, and Greet, then the pressure of it soured her gut. She was stuck between obeying her father and lying to her mother.

Which was the better option to take? Going against Vader. She didn't live with him and would only have to put up with him in a bad mood the next time she saw him, and that was a month away. With Moeder, if she was caught lying, the punishments would become more frequent. The lies about what she did for Dorothea were different, Ineke could cope with those.

"I won't lie to her," she said.

"No, I don't suppose you would. You're too good. I shouldn't have expected you to. Just…just play it down, all right? Don't be too happy about Greet when you go home. Mamma will be jealous, feel hurt and insecure in her role as your mother. She'll worry you'll like Greet more than her, and that's only natural."

That wasn't hard to imagine, although it wouldn't quite be how Vader thought. Moeder wouldn't care whether Ineke liked Greet more—unless she was Lief she wasn't bothered about Ineke's feelings—but it would mean Monster became worse, and she'd think up things for Ineke to do to upset Greet on future visits. Little missions.

For the rest of the journey, Ineke sang to Christoffel who fell asleep by the end of lullaby three. Vader parked outside a house in the Museum Quarter. Moeder said it cost a lot to live here. Greet was Vader's secretary, and Christoffel went to the nursery in the building where they worked.

Ineke clambered out and stared at the tall black house in a long row, five white-framed windows high. She'd never been here before, so this was a big step. Would Greet bark at her to take off her shoes? Would they have white carpets like at home, everything clean and bare? Or would coloured rugs be soft under her feet?

Vader took a still-sleeping Christoffel from his seat. "Come along."

The door opened, and a woman appeared. She smiled. She wasn't a pig, she wasn't even pink but light-brown, which explained why Christoffel looked like he had a slight tan. Greet's hair, all springy black coils, reached her shoulders, and she had the darkest brown eyes Ineke had ever seen. She was the opposite to Moeder, who was pale and golden, her irises blue, but Greet was much prettier. And her jeans, T-shirt, and flip-flops, something Moeder would never put on, meant she was like many of the mothers at school.

"Ineke," she said. "It's so lovely to meet you."

She held her arms out, and Ineke wasn't sure what to do. This woman, was she being like Lief, pretending she was happy to see her? Would she change into Nors as soon as Ineke did something she didn't like?

"It's okay, Ineke," Vader said.

She stepped forward and received a hug. Greet smelled of flowers, and her arms felt different to Lief's, holding her tight, as if she wanted to touch her. Unsettled by her emotions, which sprang up as a twist of anger and unfairness that Greet wasn't her mother, Ineke pulled back.

"Give her time," Vader said to his wife.

Greet took Ineke's hand and led her inside.

This house…it was everything home wasn't. They'd stepped directly into a large living room that reached to the back of the building, patio doors open, a wooden deck stretching over part of the canal. Pots of flowers lined the edges, and tall banister rails meant Christoffel wouldn't topple into the water. A green barge drifted past, the people on deck drinking bottles of beer.

Christoffel's toys lay scattered on the shiny floorboards, a big tub beside the fireplace holding more. Vader placed him on a sofa, laying cushions down his length so he didn't roll off. Had he done that to Ineke when she'd been little? Had he stared down at her like that, his smile showing his love? No, Moeder had said he hadn't loved his daughter, hadn't even wanted a child back then. She was an inconvenience to both of them.

"Would you like a drink?" Greet asked.

Ineke nodded. She was overly warm, although it was cool in here from the air-conditioning; the heat boiling her alive was jealousy in a too-hot coat. She wanted to live here, in this house with its picture-covered sage-green walls, images that showed Vader, Greet, and Christoffel smiling on beaches, on that deck, and places she didn't recognise. Where they'd been on holiday?

Ineke never went on those.

Tears prickling, she followed Greet into a kitchen, the presence of mess not the abomination Moeder had said it was but a comfort. More toys on the floor. A toaster, blender, and other things on the worktops that were in a cupboard at home, only taken out when needed. Some dirty plates sat in the sink, probably from their breakfast.

Greet went to a wide fridge-freezer hidden behind a cupboard door and took out a jug of orange juice. She poured some into a glass and popped it on the island. "Are you hungry?"

Ineke shook her head, but the fruit in the bowl called to her. Strawberries, raspberries, and bananas. She stood at the island, waiting to be told she could sit, the urge to cry too much. Her tears fell, and she wanted to run, go home where she knew the rules, where everything had a place and she understood what she was feeling. Here, she'd been bombarded with emotions she'd never experienced, and processing them seemed impossible.

"Oh, you poor thing. Come here." Greet rounded the island and wrapped Ineke up, her arms soft and wonderful.

A surge of unfairness swept through Ineke. She wanted this, yet she couldn't stand those arms around her. For one horrible moment, she thought she might scream.

"Get off *me!" she shouted, pushing the woman away, regretting her outburst but unable to take it back now. She ran to the front door. Sat on the floor, and she'd stay there with her eyes closed until Vader took her home. If she didn't see what she couldn't have, then it would be all right. She wouldn't hurt. She wouldn't have to admit that this life, this world here, wasn't for her.*

Because Vader didn't really want her in it.

Greet would think she was a horrible girl now. She wouldn't be allowed to come back after this. Why would anyone want someone like her around? She was a filthy girl who left spit on the floor, an annoying little slave no one could love. She'd made her parents unhappy by being born, so she should be punished for it. She didn't deserve to be here.

"I told you it wasn't a good idea," Vader said, likely from the kitchen. "Now you can see she can't cope with it, will you stop asking me to bring her? It's better that we go for lunch and bowling. Keep it simple. Anything more will give false hope, and I can't do that to her. I have to maintain an emotional distance. You know that."

"I wanted her to have us as a family. I know you told me everything, why you can't deal with it all, but she's just a child. She shouldn't have to pay for what her mother's done. She has no one else but us. And I wanted her to like me so much," Greet said.

"I know, but girls are funny about new mother figures. She'll be feeling torn. I know I said Evi changed after Ineke was born, but she's back to her old self now, and she's a good mother. Ineke might think she's being disloyal by letting you hug her."

"This is perfect for you."

"I won't deny it, I've never wanted my past in my life now, it's too much of a reminder of what I went through with Evi, but..."

"It's not Ineke's fault."

"I know."

"So let's make this work."

"I don't think I can, Greet. I'd better take her out. Keep things the same. Ineke likes order."

Footsteps. Ineke held her breath.

"Come on. Up you get. Stop being so silly."

Ineke opened her eyes and stood. Waited for Vader to open the door. In the car, she sat in the back, staring out of the window, moving farther and farther from the life she'd always wanted. Instead, she had a nasty mother who'd convinced Vader she was good.

"Don't take me home yet," she blurted.

"I'm not. We're going bowling."

Ineke relaxed. He was right. She did like order.

Chapter Six

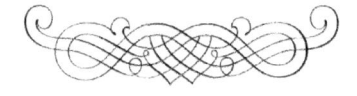

This man had made a serious mistake. Joep Bakker. A known drug dealer who shouldn't be operating on Hendrik's turf. Greased-back hair. A tan leather jacket, inappropriate for this time of year when it was so cold. It appeared new, shiny. Perhaps he'd got it for Christmas, a gift from a loved one, although from what Hendrik knew about his family, they didn't have much money. So he must have treated himself. Either way, Joep was someone who'd been brought up on the wrong side of Slotervaart, an area some would consider unsafe, the crime rate high. He didn't belong in those clothes—smart trousers and shoes that cost more than the average person could afford.

You could take the man out of the shitty streets but not the shitty streets out of the man, Hendrik knew that first-hand. There would always be a chunk of Slotervaart in *him*, too, no matter how he'd dressed his life up so it appeared he belonged in the Museum Quarter where he had a house, bought with drug money and various other things he had going on.

Joep had led his life before selling drugs as a scavenger, a no-mark who'd worked a crappy job for low pay. Underneath his new façade was still the same little bastard, desperate to become someone.

Drugs were a lucrative business. How far up the chain was he now? As far as Hendrik was aware from the last time he'd had Joep looked into, he was just a seller for some unknown man, someone Hendrik wanted to take down so he could snatch his business from under him. Joep must have climbed the ranks.

I should keep my eye on the ball more. Be up to date with things. Get Joep to tell me who he works for.

It was a struggle sometimes, to be who he wanted to be. The London leaders fascinated him. Their fame stretched all the way around the internet, articles about them if you dug deep enough. He admired their way of doing things and, desperate to do the same here, he'd embarked on this journey. He still had a lot to learn but, like Joep, he'd created a façade built over his origins and hoped he could pull it off. He'd been in trouble in the past, had escaped a prison sentence, and from then on had vowed to make something of himself. Do illegal things, just not getting caught this time.

If he were honest, Moon scared him. The man had been a leader for a long, long time, he was hardened, tough, and everything Hendrik wasn't. Still, Hendrik had done a good job, making out he was on a par, and now had Moon in his palm, a feat he hadn't thought he could engineer at first. But he had. He was growing, getting better at this.

He returned his attention to the drug dealer. Joep would be dealt with, but not before Hendrik had fun with him. He wanted answers, and he intended to get them. His research into torture had taught him how best to get information. While he wasn't *quite* used to seeing the results, he never let on that it churned his stomach. To show weakness would be his downfall.

Joep, sitting at the table in the base house, surrounded by Hendrik's armed men, shook violently. Hendrik took a seat opposite him, beneath the bare bulb that shone bright, almost too bright. It had been a long day. Hendrik had finally got over Moon's refusal now Ineke was dead. The man had proved himself, and from the moment they'd agreed to an alliance, things should have gone smoothly. And they had. Until Joep had taken the body.

"Who do you work for?" Hendrik asked.

"I can't tell you that."

"But I want to know."

"It's more than my life's worth to say."

"Interesting. So you're prepared to die to keep the person's identity safe?"

"Yeah, otherwise they'll go after my mother."

Hendrik knew a stubborn bastard when he saw one, and Joep wasn't about to open up on that subject. Maybe he would with this one. "What were you doing at the hotel?"

"Seeing a woman."

"Ah, so in a respectable place like that, you expect me to believe the type of woman staying there would be interested in entertaining the likes of *you*? The people there aren't on your level. Even the sex workers are too good for you. Pond scum, that's what you are."

It's what I am underneath it all.

He hated the dirty bitches, although he didn't mind using them to make money—they had to be good for *something*. His plan to send a load of them off to the UK meant they were no longer dirtying up Amsterdam, although Bart had rightly pointed out that more would take their place in his beloved city. Like rats, they'd swarm in, lace and silk hiding their private parts. The sex trade was too lucrative here for it to be banned. Despite that, shipping some off would calm his raging thoughts on the subject. He'd feel like he was *doing* something to clean the place up.

But it will be like shovelling snow while it's still snowing.

His mother had been a prostitute. She hadn't hidden it either, talking about it at the school gates, embarrassing him. Other mothers had given him pitying stares, and he'd wished he belonged to them instead. A life brought up by a woman who'd entertained men while he'd been at home in the next bedroom would always stay with him. The grunts, the cries, the slaps, then the thud of footsteps, the men slamming the front door on their way out. Only for it to happen all over again half an hour later. Repeat, repeat, repeat.

I'm glad she's dead.

I'm glad I killed her.

Hendrik studied Joep, hating everything he stood for. Some kid who'd tried to better himself when he shouldn't have bothered because he didn't have what it took to rise to the top. He should have remained in his place and the level of poverty he'd been born into. For some who climbed the ladder, you'd never know of their previous life, but Joep…it stood out a mile. Hendrik disregarded the fact *he'd* pulled himself up from the gutter. Maybe his dislike for Joep was because it shone a light on who Hendrik used to be—something he didn't appreciate being reminded of.

"What were you *really* doing there?" he asked.

"Look, you don't even need to know."

"Oh, I do. I need to know everything that goes on around here. In fact, I already know a lot about you. Drugs, isn't it? Although as far as I'm aware, you haven't been stupid enough to peddle them in my area. But maybe you have and I just haven't seen it. That hotel is in my jurisdiction. I can't see those who run it letting this sort of behaviour go on, so you must be doing it on the quiet. That's probably why you were in the underground car park out of the way."

"I…" Joep's shoulders slumped, as though this scenario had defeated him.

"If you don't tell me the truth, one of my men will boil your skin—and you don't want to know how that will happen, so be a good boy and answer me honestly." A rush of adrenaline sped through Hendrik. This, *this* was what he'd always wanted, to be feared, in control, someone to be respected.

Joep's eyes widened for a second—perhaps the world *boil* had frightened him—but he remained stubbornly silent. Whoever he dealt drugs for would have told him to keep his mouth shut or else. Hendrik respected his loyalty, but it wasn't going to get him very far. Just hurt. Murdered.

Hendrik waited for two minutes, counting the seconds in his head. With no response from Joep, he turned to Bart. Sighed. "Prepare for the boil."

Bart left the room.

Hendrik leaned forward. "He'll be a few minutes, so we have time for you to change your mind. What were you doing at the hotel?"

"I'm dead if I tell you."

You're dead anyway. "So what you're saying is you're more afraid of your boss than you are of me?" Hendrik gestured to his men. "Of them? *I* could hurt your mother, too." Pissed off that his name wasn't as well-known as he'd expected by now, and he wasn't someone to be scared of as far as Joep was concerned, he stuffed down the anger. He'd deal with it another day. "Tell me about the body."

"What?" Joep stared at him in shock.

"The body that was in the car park."

"I don't know about a body! God, that's got nothing to do with me."

"Funny, because you drove out of there not long after the corpse was dumped."

"I swear to you, I didn't touch it. Didn't even *see* it."

"CCTV loses you for ten minutes. What were you doing in that time?"

"What?"

"You drove from the hotel, went out of sight in Slotervaart, then emerged. Of course, you have many friends there who'd be willing to hide a body for you. And you'd know all the places you could leave her if you didn't want anyone else involved. The question is, what would you even *want* with a body? Unless you're a necrophile."

"A what?"

"Someone who is affected by the urge to have sex with dead people."

"No, no, that's not me. I'd never—"

Hendrik slammed his palm on the table. "I've had enough of your lies now. Where. Is. The. Body?"

"Please..." Joep's eyes rounded. "Oh God, what's he got in *there*?"

Bart walked over to stand beside Joep. He held a stew pan, stubby ring handles on the sides, gloves on his hands. Steam coiled from the top, and a faint *plink* sound peppered Joep's staggered breathing. One of the other men, Abel, peeled away from the corner and, using thin rope from his pocket, got on with securing Joep's wrists to the back of the chair. Joep struggled to get away.

Hendrik reached over to slap his face. "Behave! And to answer your question, it's vegetable oil." He nodded to Bart.

The devious right-hand man lifted the pot and poured a narrow stream from a spout on the side of the pan. Oil slapped onto the top of Joep's head, his scream loud and annoying, his teeth bared. Golden liquid dribbled down his face and, unable to claw at it, he stood, dashing away from Bart with the chair attached to him. Another man stepped out of the nearest corner and gripped Joep's shoulders, steering him back to the table. He forced him to sit.

"I expect that hurt quite a lot," Hendrik said.

The skin had turned red where the oil had touched his face, Joep's scalp scarlet, blistering at the point of contact. Tears streaked from the drug dealer's red-rimmed eyes, one of the lids ruined. Bart placed the pot on the table and reached into his pocket, bringing out a sandwich bag. He opened it, took a handful of salt, and dashed it into Joep's face.

The resulting scream hurt Hendrik's eardrums.

Titters went round.

Hendrik waited for the man to quiet. "So, are you prepared to talk yet?"

Joep's teeth chattered. He was probably shitting himself, fear pounding through him. "I didn't…I don't know…where…"

"Whoever you work for should be proud of you for standing by them so staunchly. There aren't many people who would keep quiet when their skin is alive with heat." Hendrik lifted his chin at Bart.

More oil, a longer pour, and Joep screeched, his teeth on show again, gums turning a lighter shade of pink. He stood, stamping his feet, fists clenched, eyes scrunched shut. His cheeks bloated, as though he'd filled his mouth with air, except it wasn't that, more the skin expanding from contact with the oil. And that skin, it was wrecked, sizzling, red, split in places. Pushed down to sitting again, Joep heaved in a huge breath, his blubbery lips swollen to twice their original size.

"I think that's enough of that."

Bart left the room. Joep cried, his sobs hoarse, perhaps with relief that the stew pot had been taken away.

"Now then, I realise that by killing you I may never know where the body is, but sometimes you just have to do these things anyway." *I'm not going to admit that you'll never tell me, that I've failed in getting it out of you.*

"No, please…"

"The time for begging is over. Unless you'd like to tell me what I want to know."

"I…the body…"

"Yes?"

"Rembrandtpark."

"That wasn't so difficult, was it. However, I don't believe you." Hendrik mused, rolling something around his mind. "I suppose it doesn't really matter *where* she is. She was just a pawn, a job that needed doing."

Bart returned. "Would you like me to do the usual?"

"That would be lovely."

Bart approached Joep, jerking his head at Abel to hold the back of the chair steady. Hendrik applied his poker face so his disgust at what was going to happen didn't show. Bart bent over and picked at the peeling skin, stripping it off to the melody of Joep's fresh screams. Skin flicked off his finger, Bart ripped off some more, almost the whole cheek covering in one go, some deeper parts coming away to reveal bloodied flesh.

Joep passed out.

Bart wandered out again, his part in this over.

Hendrik sighed. "String him up."

He walked into the kitchen, Bart already making him the required Earl Grey tea. A cup of that was always welcome after such a distasteful event.

"Do you think he took her?" Bart asked.

"Why would Moon lie and say someone stole her? He knows that would be a stupid thing to do when he's not on home soil."

"But why would Joep even *want* the body?"

"Maybe he thought whoever he was selling drugs to in the car park would think he'd done it, so he took her away to hide her. Or maybe it's as I said, necrophilia. Either way, do we really care? She's dead and not our problem anymore—and we both know she should have been killed days ago because that's what I was told to do. We made a point, that I did it on *my* terms, in *my* time."

"But you told…you told the one pulling your strings that Ineke was already dead, so they don't even know you *made* a point."

Hendrik wasn't prepared to discuss that. So long as *he* knew he'd had control and not the string-puller, that was all that mattered. "When you collect Moon tomorrow, tell the hotel her room isn't needed."

Bart chuckled. "She must have thought she'd hit the jackpot being put in there."

Hendrik smiled. "Just proves how wrong she was, doesn't it. I had to hide her because, well, you know why."

"Shame she had to go. She'd have brought in a lot of revenue in the UK. Men would be clamouring for her. They'd pay extra for a Dutch girl."

That got Hendrik's back up. "Are you questioning my decisions? Like I had a *choice* in whether she died or not?"

"No."

"Good."

Hendrik took the tea and went down into the basement, bypassing the room Joep was being hanged in. He'd think about where to put his body tomorrow. Towards the back of the corridor, he unlocked the larger room and entered. Closed the door. Flicked the light on. Faces, twelve of them, pale, all showing sleepy expressions from where he'd woken them, then fear. Twelve beds in a row. Twelve nightstands.

"Someone is coming tomorrow. You need to be dressed and ready by one. Makeup, hair, everything. I want you to look pretty." He jabbed a thumb in the direction of a vanity unit holding everything they needed, a wardrobe full of lingerie in various sizes, and the door to a primitive bathroom. "Behave, make him want to take you to England, and you'll be rewarded."

"I don't want to go anymore," one of them whispered.

Hendrik couldn't work out who'd said it, and annoyance roared through him. "Tough. You agreed, and you must abide by that."

Like I fucking had to with Ineke.

He walked out, twisting the key, satisfied by the clunk of the lock.

Chapter Seven

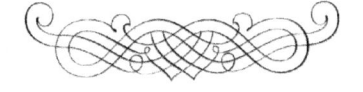

Schiphol Airport was pretty busy. Men in suits swinging briefcases dodged around those on holiday for a bit of weed-riddled partying. George struggled to get his head around people flying to work and back each day, although the flight hadn't been long. It seemed they'd no sooner sat and buckled up than they were there.

Neither of them had time to catch a quick kip, so George was a bit grumpy, not to mention uneasy that they may have to do some sorting in Amsterdam. He didn't like not having familiarity around him, he preferred to be in complete control, and without their copper, Janine, to help smooth the way, he felt a little adrift.

Janine. She'd dropped the bombshell she was pregnant and they needed to get a new bent copper. She'd suggested Bryan Flint, so Mason, their private investigator, currently had the job of digging up dirt on the bloke. Hopefully something could be found, a tidbit to bribe him with, forcing him into working for them. Mind you, Janine had said he was the only one she reckoned would be fit for turning, so maybe Flint would walk into their welcome arms without a quibble. Regardless, it was always good to have insurance, and anyway, they'd video him in the warehouse, involved in a future murder, and use that against him like they had with Janine.

A shame she was leaving them. He'd grown fond of her, plus he'd got used to how they worked together. It had been difficult to transition from DI Rod Clarke to her, learning her ways, what buttons to push, and now they were going to have to do it again.

Maybe Flint will suit us better. I bet he's not a moody fucker like her.

But that was something to deal with once they got home. For now, he'd have to be on his A game, absolutely no fuck-ups on Dutch soil. No going at it, a loose cannon. He'd be relying on Greg to keep him in line more than usual. And his other personalities were *not* welcome here. He couldn't risk Mad or Ruffian making an appearance.

At the baggage claim, they waited for their small cases then followed the signs to leave, waiting in a queue. Several people tacked onto the sides of it, which pissed him the hell off. Where was the British way where you never butted in unless you had a death wish and the line was one or two people wide?

"Fuck's sake," he muttered, checking they were being funnelled into the correct area. Two signs, one for UK passports, another for everyone else. "Bloody Brexit. We're now singled out like lepers."

The wait wore on, a northern woman behind telling her daughter no, she couldn't get her eyebrows threaded, and no, she'd never fit into a size ten dress because of her puppy fat, and no, she wasn't allowed to stay out past eight o'clock. George turned around to give her a filthy look, but the woman stared back as though *he* was the one in the wrong.

"Some people need to mind their own business," she said to her child.

"Some people need to stop body-shaming their kids," he snapped back. "She's fine the size she is, leave her alone."

"Ah, piss off, you nosy bastard."

I'm not in London now, I'm not in London now. Don't react.

He faced the other way. Clenched a fist around his suitcase handle, dying to say something cutting that would take her down a peg. He was already riled up, trying to cope with being in another country, this bloody stupid queue, and that woman wasn't helping matters.

"Don't," Greg whispered.

"But did you hear her?"

"Yeah, and *she'll* hear *you* if you don't keep your voice down."

"I don't care if she does."

"What part of 'let's get this done without drawing attention to ourselves' don't you understand?"

"Whatever, knobhead."

"Is that you saying you agree I made a valid point?"

"Might be."

Just as they reached the part of the line where they'd be herded into a cordoned-off maze of two sections, a woman in a uniform came by.

"You're in the wrong place for UK," she called and pointed to her right.

George looked for another ceiling sign that would tell him where she meant, but there wasn't one.

"Where do we need to go?" he asked her.

"Down there."

"I realise that, but *where*?"

She rolled her eyes at him, then moved on.

Greg nudged him. "Calm down. We'll find it."

"But everyone's swarming that way now, and we'll have lost our place in the fucking queue." Mad George nudged to come out, but he shoved him back into his box. Losing his shit would only make things worse, especially running round this airport, punching people to relieve his temper.

Northern Bird tutted and barged past, her case bashing into George's. He had to fight off the urge to slap the side of her head. Instead, he gawped at her back, the daughter peering over her shoulder as if to say sorry, which went some way to alleviating his anger. Some people needed a clout round the earhole, and that woman was one of them.

They followed the exodus, went through the checks, and eventually made it outside, confronted with a huge sign on the ground, each letter individual and higher than a person: I amsterdam, the 'I am' red, the rest white. The absence of a capital A got right on his nerves, but he squashed it down. He wasn't here to pick fault but to get Moon the fuck out of the Netherlands, and he'd do well to remember their reason for leaving London at the drop of a hat. Before that, if it was possible and they wouldn't get caught, he planned to fuck Hendrik Alderliesten over, teach him that messing with a London leader had consequences.

At least Moon was free now, let out of wherever he'd been trapped. They'd find out more when they met up with him, but for now they had to collect a vehicle from Europcar and get to the hotel.

Presented with a gleaming black SUV, George smiled. He dumped their cases in the back and got in, setting the satnav to English. Their hotel was a few minutes away.

Greg sat in the passenger seat. "I'll doctor the plate and whatever later. I brought some black tape with me. And good luck driving on the wrong side of the road with your temper."

George frowned. "Do you want to drive?"

"Might be best."

"Fucking Nora."

They swapped places, finally getting on the road. At the hotel, they checked in, their rooms on the fourth floor. George went into his, put his case on a weird ladder contraption hanging on the wall—*after* he'd Googled what the chuff it was—and got changed. They'd agreed to ditch their usual grey suits and red ties for black tracksuits. Along with the fake beards and glasses, and trainers instead of their polished shoes, they should appear sufficiently different to when they'd arrived. He slapped his beard on, laced up his trainers, briefly contemplating the receptionist wondering who the hell they were when they next left, but this place was so big, maybe she wouldn't take any notice.

He messaged Moon.

GG: WE'RE AT THE HOTEL.

MOON: WHAT ROOM ARE YOU IN? I'LL COME AND SEE YOU.

George told him, then went next door, tapping on Greg's door.

His brother opened it and stared. "I was just going to the loo, bruv."

"Hurry up. And get your trackies on. Moon's on the way."

Back in his own room, George left his door ajar and walked to the window. It faced the main road, a tram gliding along to stop and pick up passengers from beneath a plastic awning. The kid in him wanted to have a ride on one, to see some sights and actually have a break from Cardigan, but he doubted they'd have time for dicking about. It would have been nice, though. Maybe, if all went well and there wasn't a massive need to leave Amsterdam quickly, he could persuade Greg to visit the main city.

Greg thudded in and flopped on the bed. "I'm knackered." He yawned loudly.

George resisted yawning himself. "Didn't you sleep much?"

"No."

"Me neither. After that message from Debbie last night, then going over things for Ichabod to watch the Estate while we're gone… Then there's Janine's pregnancy issue. I got about two hours in the end. My mind wouldn't shut up."

"The same as your gob sometimes, then."

"Only you could say that and get away with it. I'm that annoyed by that cow at the airport, if you were anyone else, I'd deck you just so I felt better."

"You need to watch yourself."

"Yeah, I'm aware of that."

A knock at the door had George stiffening, even though he was expecting it. He strode to answer it. Moon stood in the corridor, his face more weathered than usual, his normal air of bluster somewhat diminished. It was a shock to see him like this, to be honest, and George bit back telling him he looked like shit.

"All right, mate?" he said instead.

"No, I'm fucking not. Would you be? Christ." Moon came in and went straight to the window, glancing left then right. "I'm paranoid they're watching me after the stunt I pulled."

Jesus wept. "What stunt?" George shut the door and eyed the kettle. "Hang on." He filled it in the bathroom then put it on to boil. "Go on. Start from the beginning, but don't go all round the houses. Condensed version, please."

Moon sat on a nearby chair. "Don't boss me about. I've had enough of that from Hendrik. I came back because he wanted to apologise in person. I quite fancied seeing him grovel, not to mention smoking weed again, living it large. My ego had a hand in that. And before you say anything, yes, it needs seeing to. Anyway, he offered for me to do that job again, didn't he, and—"

"Stop," George said. "You're acting like we know what you came here for in the first place. You just said it was business. What job?"

Moon appeared shifty. Guilty. Ashamed. "Taking girls to the UK and making them work. Basically trafficking."

"Fucking hell!"

"Don't assume I think it's okay. Hear me out. I said no the first time, and he didn't like it. Got shirty with me. I went home, then he rings to say could I come back, he's sorry. So I got on a flight, went to see him, and he locked me in a room for fuck knows how long. Took my phone. Some pleb called Bart fed me and brought water, and I had a shower and toilet in there, so that was something, but fuck me, I thought I'd never get out."

"You said they took your phone, but you were texting Debbie while you were away, she told us."

"It was them."

"That explains why you kept it short and sweet, saying you were too busy to talk. Deb thought you were just being an ignorant wanker to be honest."

"Bastards, they are. Anyway, Bart came to my room, and some commotion or other was going on downstairs, so he ran out, leaving my door open—what a fucking rookie, eh? I nipped into the office along the landing, found my phone, and got hold of Debbie."

"Why didn't you leave the bloody house?"

"Because some crabby cunt stood at the bottom of the stairs with a gun. So, before you rudely butted in..." Moon gave him one of his trademark glares. "I was on my way back to my room when Bart caught me. He fired his fucking gun, didn't he. I waited for the bullet to hit, thought I was a goner, but it must have just been a warning. I made out I'd come to help him with whatever was going on downstairs. So, long story short, I agreed to run the girls for Hendrik—it was the only way I could see myself getting away from there."

"What happened next?"

"This is the bit that could have landed me right in the shit. They told me I had to kill someone for them as insurance. Take a picture of myself with the dead body and send it to them—Bart gave me my phone back and some instructions, plus a burner. I had to go to the room next to mine. Turns out there's this bird in there, Ineke, and she'd been threatened that if she didn't go to England, her little brother would be bumped off, and he's only ten. As you can imagine, I wasn't fucking impressed, and I didn't want to kill her."

"Please tell me you didn't," Greg said.

"Of course not!" Moon huffed. "What do you take me for?" He went on to explain what he'd done, Ineke going along with it. "So I told Bart someone nicked the body. Bart gets hold of me, saying they've caught the driver and will deal with him. God fucking help me, I should feel sorry for the poor bastard, but I'm just relieved it worked out in my favour."

"What if he says he didn't take her?"

"I'll cross that bridge when I come to it."

"What's the score now?" Greg asked.

"They're coming for me at one. Want me to choose some girls. Bart sent a message this morning to say the meeting is at the house."

Greg narrowed his eyes. "What if that's a trick?"

"I thought the same, but you're here, so if I don't come out of that house in two hours, you go in."

"Where there's a crabby cunt with a gun and we have no weapons?" George pointed out. "Right. That sounds all kinds of perfect."

"Don't be so bloody sarcastic." Moon switched topics, conveniently, and mentioned a bit about Ineke's life.

George winced. Poor cow. "So it makes total sense why she'd agree to work for Hendrik—she's used to being controlled."

"Yeah, but she doesn't want to be anymore. New start an' all that. Now, if we can kill Hendrik and his men—there's only six altogether, plus a driver—then she can come home with us and not have to worry about Christoffel."

"That's the brother?"

"Yeah."

"And how the hell are we going to be able to do that without getting caught?"

"The house is in one of the backstreets, no CCTV. I know there are no cameras because he bragged about it, which is why he has his base there. I didn't see any either time I was there. It's a rough part of the city where no fucker takes any notice of what's going on. No twitching nets, know what I mean? The whole street looks abandoned anyway."

George sat on the bed. "So what do we do with them after? It's not like I can dump them in the canal, is it. It's not the bastard Thames, and I don't want to be seen buying a saw to chop them up—and come to think of it, where would I even do that? I doubt there's a warehouse going begging."

Moon smiled. "Some houses here have basements. I Googled it. Anyway, if we leave the lot of them down there, the smell won't be so bad. I'd rather we had plastic sheeting to hand so we can wrap them up, but it's too big a risk to buy any."

"Right. How prominent is Hendrik? Will his absence be noticed?"

"I expect so, but I don't think he's as tough as he makes out. He's a leader of sorts, but nothing like us where everyone knows. More like some half-rate gangster who reckons he's all that."

"Yet you told us he was a hotshot."

"That's what he led me to believe."

"How do you plan for us to get in there?" George had to boil the kettle again because he'd been so engrossed in Moon's story.

"I've got a plan."

George got on with making coffee. "Right, well, tell us about it, because we're not going in blind, then I want to meet Ineke, see if she's on the level."

"Not a problem." Moon's usual demeanour had returned. Maybe he felt better now they were here. Bolstered. Confident. He smiled. "So, this is how I hope it pans out…"

Chapter Eight

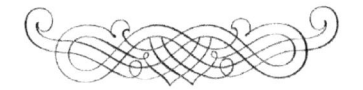

Moon was right. The twins *were* massive, and they *did* look scary. It was difficult to see their mouths because of their thick beards. Were they a disguise along with the glasses? The one who'd introduced himself as George sat on a chair by her window and stretched his legs out. The other sat on one side of the bed, Moon the other. Ineke lowered herself to the chair at the desk, shaking a little from their presence, their black clothing giving them a thuggish vibe. She'd been with countless men in her time, some of them frightening in a violent, sexual way, but none of them had been as mesmerising. There was something about these two that got to her. Had Moeder felt that way with Vader? Starstruck, in awe, imagining what it would be like to be with him for the rest of her life?

Shaking off the weird attraction, Ineke waited for one of them to speak. Which one would lead? Who was the more dominant?

"Moon's told us a bit about you," George said, answering her silent questions. "I want to get this clear straight off the bat. Are you *sure* you want to come to London?"

She nodded; she had to do this, break away, throw off the final link of the chain that bound her to this place. She couldn't stick around anymore, not since Hendrik had added to her unhappiness here. Maybe Amsterdam was unlucky for her. London could be the key to all of her dreams. "I need to get away. The memories…there are too many. Greet, my stepmother, she came to the window of my room at night and held up cards she had written on, asking me to stop, to let her take care of me. She does not know that nothing she does can fix what happened—she does not even *know* what happened to me. If I stay, she will always find me."

He frowned. "What, she was taking a gander at you in your *flat*? What a weirdo."

"No, the room I worked in."

It seemed to take him a moment to remember where he was. In Amsterdam, where women could stand in windows on display and not be arrested for what they were offering. It had never been a shock to Ineke, she'd grown up knowing this, and although people around the world knew what went on here, she supposed it was still a shock when confronted with it.

"Oh," he said. "In the Red Light District."

"Yes."

"What about your old dear?"

Ineke didn't understand. "Old dear?"

"Mother. Where is she?"

Ineke closed her eyes. In her mind's eye, Lief swayed to music, then Monster took over, ripping the cushions off the sofa and throwing them around, shouting that her daughter was a fucking little bitch. The afternoon Ineke had got back from Vader's house had been a terrible time. One of the worst.

She opened her eyes again and stared at the floor. "She…she still lives in the house where I grew up."

"Moon told us a bit about her. She's a bitch and a half. Needs dealing with. Or at the very least she owes you an apology. I mean, getting you to lick the floor? Fucking disgusting. I should string her up and whip the shit out of her. Batter her until she can't breathe. Slice her tits off and—"

"George!" Greg barked.

"Well…" George shook his head. "Makes my blood boil the way some kids are treated."

Alarmed by his outburst—it reminded her of Monster—Ineke blinked in the hope it would cool her hot eyes. "The floor was clean."

George gawped at her. "Pardon me? Are you saying it was *okay* because it wasn't dirty?"

"I…" She wasn't sure how to respond to such an angry man. She thankfully recognised it was on her behalf, but still, what should she say?

"She's been through enough without you mouthing off," Moon said.

George glanced at his brother. "She needs to see Vic as soon as possible. We have to fix this."

Ineke's stomach rolled over. "Who is that?"

"Our therapist." George twiddled his beard. "You need to talk through this, to understand it wasn't okay to lick the floor. None of it was your fault, and I'm fucking steaming about it. I want to slice your mother's face up and stab her in the cunt."

She hid her second slap of shock—at what he wanted to do *and* someone caring about her mental health. Vader would say she had to get on with it, cope by herself, never let anyone know her weak spots—but then he still didn't know what she'd been through.

Now she was older, would he believe her? Now she didn't have the threat of being taken away, locked in a cupboard and starved, could she tell him? Would he want to know now he didn't have to be responsible for her like he would if she'd told him as a child? Moeder had said Vader wouldn't be allowed to take her if she was arrested for abuse, that she'd make up a story and say he was horrible to her, and the children's home would snatch her before he could, but that had been a lie.

Like so many things.

Was there any point in revealing everything to Vader? Maybe. It would perhaps make him feel guilty for believing Lief, that she was good and kind, that he hadn't probed deeper to find out if anything bad was going on—that he hadn't even wanted to. Those hours she'd spent with him once a month had to be endured by him, that had become more obvious the older she'd become, and he certainly wouldn't want to entertain tales of the abuse now. No, his time for being with her was over. She was an adult, not his problem.

But Greet, she'd listen. She'd want to make it all better. Sometimes she'd visited the school at playtime, bringing Christoffel in the pushchair so Ineke could see him—Vader hadn't brought him much when they went bowling. Greet had asked if she was all right, said Ineke could tell her anything if she wanted to. Ineke had remained quiet, she couldn't risk Monster finding out, but once, she'd wanted to spit it all out, ask Greet to take her away. Hide her in the tall black house.

Why could I never let her step in and be my mother, even after I left home? Why did it still feel such a betrayal to Lief and all of her other personalities?

A therapist *was* probably the best way forward. Someone who wasn't involved, who didn't know the players. She should take the offer, get help to understand why she'd hadn't spotted the signs in Hendrik—after all, he was made from the same mould as Monster. But was this, what these three men were prepared to do for her, like Moeder had said? That if it looks too good to be true… They were promising Ineke a new world. Should she believe them? The way George had spoken about the floor—yes, he was disgusted, it wasn't an act, but a small part of her warned Ineke to remain on her guard. Hendrik had seemed sincere, yet he'd set her up to die.

"I would like that, to see this Vic," she said. "How much will it cost?"

"Nothing." George scrubbed a hand down his face.

She laughed bitterly. "There is always a price."

"Not with us, unless we say so. If I tell you it's free, it's fucking free. I can't let you go out into the world with all that crap in your head. You deserve a nice life, one without blame. I bet someone's told you that, haven't they, that it's your fault?"

"How did you know?"

"We see it a lot, love. We help loads of people. Can't stand injustice." George glanced at the bag of food from the bakery that Moon had bought for her this morning. "I saw a pizza place on the way here. Fancy one?"

She gave him a small smile. "Yes, please."

He was one of life's carers, despite what he wanted to do to Moeder. He was kind yet awful. Was he like her mother, changing into other sides of himself?

"I'll go and get it, then. What toppings do you want?"

"Just cheese, thank you." She couldn't have anything else because Monster said it was greedy. "And pepperoni. And mushrooms." There, she'd made another stand. Fought her indoctrinated thoughts and won.

George strode out, and his brother got up to stare out of the window.

"Don't mind him," Greg said. "Bark's worse than his bite. His heart's in the right place, it's just sometimes he doesn't know when to keep his thoughts to himself. You might not even *want* him to hurt your mother. The thing with George is, his answer to everything is either violence or throwing money at people to make their lives better. In his eyes, your mother needs to be removed from your life because he knows how it feels to have a parent who…isn't nice, and what it's like when they're no longer around. I'm the same. We were both free when our fathers…died."

"You had two?" she asked.

"Long story. Maybe I'll tell you one day. For us it was a godsend they were dead, but for others in the similar boat, they can't hack the guilt of knowing they said yes to having someone killed. In London, we even give people the choice of whether to watch or not."

"Watch you *kill*?"

"Yeah. Sounds bad, but… Anyway, I expect George will offer you the same. He'll even ask if you want to do it yourself."

Ineke shook her head. "I cannot kill her. I've thought about it a hundred times but would never do it. She is… She needs help. I now know she had post-natal depression after I was born. She has never recovered. She has split personalities."

Moon laughed. "So does Georgie boy, but it doesn't mean it's okay what she did to you. Don't excuse her behaviour. That was on her."

So I was right. George has many sides to him.

Ineke had read about not taking the blame, but seeing the words and them actually penetrating her brain were two different things. When she'd left home, she was halfway to accepting she wasn't at fault, had taken the big step in removing herself from the abuse and never going back. What would it be like to see Moeder again after two years? If Ineke took the twins with her, her mother would be Lief, charming and the perfect hostess. She'd never turn into Monster in front of them.

Would they still believe me if they saw her? Heard her?

"She is good at hiding who she really is. Maybe she has given up the drink since I left. Or she could have got worse. Sometimes she threatened to kill herself, crying all the time, but I know she is still alive because I have seen her in articles. She is a judge."

Greg tutted. "Fuck me, someone who should know better."

Moon grunted. "Corrupt, the lot of them. Anyone in those sorts of establishments are."

"There have to be *some* good ones," Ineke said. "Not everyone can be bad." She refused to believe there weren't genuinely nice people around.

Moon shrugged. "Yeah, well, in my experience, they're tossers. Think they're above everyone else."

Greg watched whatever was going on outside, his eyebrows drawing together. He pinched his chin. "There's some bloke in the tram stop, staring up at me. Or maybe not me but the hotel."

"Stay there, Ineke." Moon got up and peered down from behind the protection of the voiles. "One of Hendrik's men. The crabby cunt with the gun."

Ineke hugged herself, fear poking at her. "What is he doing here? Do you think they know I am not dead?"

"Who'd tell them?" Moon came away to sit on the bed. "Do you really think they would even imagine I'd go to all that trouble with the makeup? Nah, they'd expect me to just do you in."

"Maybe he's the one who's been sent to pick you up, Moon," Greg said.

"Then he can wait. Bart said one o'clock, and I want some pizza. I had a croissant on the way back from the bakery, but all that exercise has got me hungry. Don't tell Debbie. She's banned me from eating crap. Says I need to eat healthier."

"What are you going to do? Later?" Ineke asked. "I...I am better if I know what might happen. I do not like surprises."

Moon told her his plan. "So if you just sit tight until it's all over... And remember, if you don't hear from us, get hold of Debbie so she can book your flight to get you out of here."

"And if it all goes okay, then what?"

Moon fiddled with the cigar poking up from the front pocket of his suit jacket. "You can decide whether you want to see your mother, go and say goodbye to your dad and brother, and Greet. Then it's London. I'll pay for your ticket."

Greg spoke without looking away from the outside view. "No, *we* will. And no, you don't have to pay it back. We don't deal in people trafficking and never will. We'll sort you a job if you don't want to work for Debbie, and you can rent one of our flats."

A lump filled Ineke's throat. "Why are you doing this?"

Greg finally turned her way. "Let's just say my brother likes cheering for the underdog and I go along for the ride."

"Or to keep him out of trouble," Moon muttered.

"Yeah, that an' all." Greg smiled. "Trust us. We'll get you sorted."

He winked at her.

And Ineke thought she might be in love. Just a little bit.

Chapter Nine

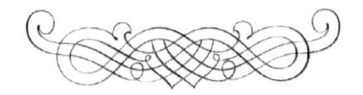

Vader stood on the doorstep. In the foyer, Ineke took her shoes off, putting them away. She'd gone straight into do-as-you're-told mode the second she'd come home. At least she recognised that. But how could she not? Her stiffening body, nerves tight, and the expectation of what was to come were a big indication. It was times like this she realised she wasn't as tense with Vader as she'd thought. He was the

preferable person to be with, despite him being prickly, and because she knew his rules, she still had that feeling of safety. He'd ruined that by taking her to his house, but she would get over it.

She waited for Lief's usual best behaviour to appear. It didn't take long.

"Won't you come in?" Lief asked, all sweet and cheerful. She fiddled with her hair at the side, twirling it round and round a finger, one hand on the edge of the door, one foot on the floor, the other with her toes pointing to it.

"No, what I've got to say can be said here."

Oh God, he's going to tell her he took me to the black house. Maybe he thinks it's better if he says it.

"Oh? That sounds a little ominous." Lief tinkled out a laugh.

Ineke closed the cupboard door and stood in front of it, palms to the wood. Ahead, a large mirror on the wall, so she looked into it. Vader and Lief were visible, so she could see their expressions. He seemed apprehensive.

"We went to my house," he said and cleared his throat. "Greet wanted to meet her."

A smile stretched. "How lovely! I'm sure they got along well. Ineke is so good, she wouldn't have been any trouble."

"She was uncomfortable, so we didn't stay long. Barely five minutes, in fact. I think she felt guilty for being with another mother figure. Like she was going against you in some way."

"Of course, but she'll get used to it. Unless you've reconsidered my offer. Why don't we stop all this silliness and you come back. Greet will learn to cope with Christoffel by herself. I should know, I did it with Ineke."

Vader sighed. "Stop this. I love Greet. I'd never leave her."

Lief's smile remained in place. "You loved me *once, but you still left. Why was that?"*

Vader's eyebrows scrunched together. "You know why."

"I wasn't well."

"No, but you've pulled yourself out of it. Move on, please. It's been too many years for us to start again now. And I don't want to. It took me a long time to get over you and what you did, but I have. I suggest you do the same."

"I don't wany anyone else."

"That's not what I heard."

Lief's smile faltered. "What do you mean?"

"Friday nights in the city. With men you've previously sent to prison. You need to be careful. It's reckless, doing that."

"I don't know what you're talking about."

"Don't play games, Evi. You've been seen."

"Who by?"

"I'm not telling you their name. A mutual colleague who's concerned. I'm just giving you a friendly warning because of your career. You don't want a slipup to ruin it. And those men, they're not exactly the right type to be around your daughter."

Your daughter. Not ours.

Ineke let the prickle of hurt grow and fester.

Another tinkle of laughter. "It sounds like a threat, not a warning."

"I would never threaten you, and you know that. Please don't twist things."

"That was my perception, and you can't control that—it's the one thing you can't rule over. You used to try hard to do it, but I never let you completely take me over."

"Put that down to perception again, as I never ruled you."

"Oh, you did, but in subtle ways. It's affected me more than you know. How I behave, the things I say…"

"To whom?"

To me, Vader. Me.

Lief ran a hand through her hair to tidy the tangle she'd created by twirling. "Let's not argue. Are you sure you don't want to come in? I have some bread in the oven. I know how much you like home-baked bread."

"I'm sure. I'll pick Ineke up next month. Please be careful how you conduct yourself. You know as well as anyone what happens to children whose parents choose the wrong path. Hanging around with ex-criminals…not a good look."

"I don't need policing."

"Yes, well…"

"So I can't tempt you? The bread?"

"No, you can't."

"I wish I could change things."

"You can't. It's done and dusted. You made your bed. Goodbye."

Lief stayed in the doorway until the noise of Vader's engine dwindled to nothing. She closed the front door, shot Ineke a look, and strutted past her, disappearing into the kitchen.

As Ineke hadn't been given any instructions, she went with the tried-and-tested option of doing the laundry. Lief would be drinking now, getting herself worked up, and when Monster had taken over, she'd appear.

It happened quicker than usual. Ineke had only just put the first load of washing into the dryer, going into the living room to keep out of the way, when Monster ran in, screeching, gripping the sides of her hair.

"When were you going to tell me about seeing Greet? If your father hadn't, were you going to keep it quiet? Keep a nasty little secret from me?" She grabbed an ornament off the sideboard, a female figurine, and threw it at the wall. It smashed and fell to the floor, its head snapped clean off, rocking to and fro. She stared at Ineke, fists clenched by her sides, eyes wide and blazing, cheeks red. "Did you like her? Love her? Is she better than me? Do you prefer the brown pig to the pink one you live with? Do you?"

Ineke didn't answer.

Monster came towards her, arms out, and snatched a seat cushion off the sofa. She chucked it, sending it careening into another ornament on a wall shelf. It toppled but had a soft landing on the recliner chair. "You're a fucking bitch. A horrible little girl who shouldn't even be here. You're ugly and rotten and ruined my life." She lifted another cushion and lobbed it.

Ineke got up and plastered her back to the wall beside the door. She couldn't leave, that would be wrong. She had to watch this play out as a punishment, to make her understand that she *made her mother like this.*

Monster grabbed the final cushion, and instead of launching it across the room, she fell to her knees and yanked the zip across. Dug her hands inside to rip the flimsy covering on the interior foam, gouging and biting pieces off, tossing them behind her. She screeched all the while, her face streaked with tears, and once she'd destroyed the foam, she let the outer cover go. Sobbed. Stared at the ceiling and mumbled that Vader had wrecked her by leaving. She shot up and staggered into the kitchen. Something glass shattered, then another, another, and Ineke trembled.

"I hate you, child!" she shouted. "I wish Dorothea would take you away and drown you like she did to those mangy cats and dogs."

Startled, Ineke swallowed down the glut of fear. Dorothea killed animals?

"I'd help her. I'd shove your head under the water and keep it there until you died."

Ineke imagined that, but it wasn't difficult to. She'd often sink beneath the surface of the bathwater, holding her breath to see what it would be like to die under there. Once, she let water in through her mouth, into her lungs, and her stupid body had responded, wanting to save her, to bring her back to this hideous life where she suffered.

"Moeder says to get in here and clean up the glass."

Ineke obeyed, entering the kitchen. Monster sat on the floor, a large shard held against her wrist.

"This would be better than taking tablets," she whispered. Verdrietig had taken over. "There'd be blood, so much of it, and the police would think you killed me. You'd be taken to that care home and put in a cupboard. You'd never be let out. You'd die in there!"

Ineke remained silent. If she spoke out of turn, it would become even worse.

Verdrietig pressed the pointed end of the shard into her skin. A bead of blood surged up around it, and she stared, as if pleased with what she'd done. "One slice, that's all it would take. I don't belong here. I don't fit. I should kill myself. No one would miss me. You're not even trying to help! To stop me!"

Because I don't want Monster to come back and hurt me if I do.

"You'll see living with me isn't so bad when you get to where you're going after I'm gone. Your father doesn't want you, that's why he won't come back. It's your *fault he left me. Why did I have to have you? Why didn't I listen when he said he wasn't ready for kids? Why did I have to have it my way?" She sniffled. "What are you looking at, you devil slave?"*

Ineke glanced at the floor. All the glass.

"I told you to clean up."

No, Monster had, but maybe Moeder didn't realise she became all these different people. Was that why she was supposed to take tablets? She'd stopped, saying she didn't need them, but she really did.

Ineke went to the cupboard and took out a broom. She swept carefully around Verdrietig, careful not to get too close, so she wasn't within slapping distance, and scooped the pieces up into a dustpan. She put the things away and took the hoover out—that would be the only way to make sure all the glass was gone, but some still glistened around Verdrietig, afternoon sunlight coming in through the window. Ineke wanted to ask her to get up, but she didn't dare.

"Oh God, I'm so sorry… I'm a wicked mother. You don't deserve this." Lief had come at last. She dropped the shard and stood, shaking the glass off her dress, stepping over the fragments and going out the back

onto the deck. She'd probably sit and watch the canal, the barges, and calm down.

Ineke finished cleaning then made tea. She carried it out to Lief who took it and placed it on a patio table then grasped Ineke's wrist gently and drew her closer. Pulled down onto her mother's lap, Ineke sank into the embrace, Lief's words floating above her.

"I'll never do this again. I'll get help, I promise. I'm a monster."

Blood from her wrist smeared Ineke's arm. Jolted by Lief's soft sobs, Ineke stared out at the canal and all the people on their decks, enjoying their drama-free Saturday. A family ate around a table, laughing and talking. Ineke had never experienced that, except at school, where she pretended to fit in. What would it be like to live like it for real, to never be worried about keeping things secret? To have a mother who didn't change into other people?

To live with Greet and forget she even had *a mother?*

"Up you pop," Lief said, bright. "I'll go and have a shower, put a plaster on my arm, and then we can go out for waffles, yes?"

Ineke nodded and clambered off her lap. At least in public she'd be safe, unless Monster came back to pinch her if she did something wrong. But cake sounded good, and for the time they were out, she could pretend again.

That Moeder loved her.

Chapter Ten

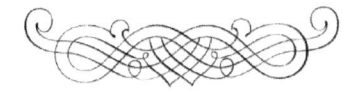

Bart had collected Moon from the hotel, the journey so far silent save for the rumble of the engine and the traffic passing by, the occasional *ting-ting* of a bike bell filtering through. Those bikes had got on his tits whenever he'd been out and about. He'd forgotten this lot drove on the wrong side of the road, too, so when he'd stepped out to cross, he'd nearly always been mowed down by some bastard cycling. A woman ahead rode along with her kids in a kind of plastic cart attached to the back of her bike. He'd have loved that as a lad.

Moon had been allowed in the front seat again, like he had on his first visit here, his former status returned to him, treated properly instead of like a criminal in the back. Did that mean his thoughts on all this being one massive trick were wrong? Or was this a part of it, maintaining the illusion that they trusted him now when they didn't? Was Hendrik playing mind games? Trying to give Moon a false sense of security? What was in store for him at the house? He hated not knowing. Like Ineke, he was better when he knew what lay ahead.

Where was the scraggly young driver? It was odd; the fact the scrote wasn't here had Moon's mind going ten to the dozen. Had they only used the driver so Bart could have walloped Moon if he didn't do as he was told when they'd taken him to the hotel last night?

He opted to break into the weird, awkward quiet. He needed to know where all the players were today for this plan to work. Mr Scraggle not being in the picture, and not knowing when he'd pop up again, was a worry. "How come you're driving? Where's the other bloke from last night?"

"He's...he could not be trusted."

"Oh. Bit of a pisser, that, when you find out some of your men are a bit...well, arseholes. Been there a few times myself. What did he do?"

"Dabbled with one of the women."

Moon feigned indignance. "Oh, that's not on, they're a bloody commodity, not there to give freebies. I take it he wasn't given permission."

"No." A muscle in Bart's jaw flickered.

"Hendrik deal with him, did he?"

"Yes, he gave the order. He is dead."

One down, six to go. "Blimey. So did he go to see the women after you two dropped me off or summat?"

"He did. We all have a key to the room. He used his unwisely."

"Seems a bit weird to me that a driver got a key."

"Hendrik wants us all to feel like we are trusted, even the driver."

"And he betrayed him. Serves himself right, then. He deserves to be dead."

Bart glanced across at him for a moment, his scowl dark and wicked. "Anyone who refuses Hendrik does."

Moon picked up on what the bloke *hadn't* said. "You don't agree with him giving me another chance?"

"No. You refused him—twice—and now suddenly you are okay with us. It is suspicious."

"I can see how you'd think that, but I realised what a dick I'd been, that's all. My girlfriend runs women. I don't hold that against her, so I was being a cock by saying pimping girls is wrong. All right, it isn't my thing, but it will be, I'll get used to it. Besides, I want to go home. Doing this for Hendrik means I get to do that."

"Just as I thought. You agreed so you would be set free."

"Something like that. We all have crosses to bear, don't we, and being a pimp will be mine if that's what Hendrik wants. I mean, he knows where I live, that my girlfriend's all but moved in and is sometimes there on her own—he could send someone to kill her if he wanted to. I don't want any harm coming to her, so I'm prepared to do as I'm told." That should do it, make Bart think he was scared of his boss. "Men like him... I don't want to get on his bad side."

"A sensible conclusion, although *you* are a man like him and could do just as much damage to Hendrik should he visit you in London. You would have your gang on your side to help you dispose of him."

"What? You're saying I plan to kill him? Where's that come from?"

"Just an observation. Hendrik is not the only one to have done his research on you. You could go back on the agreement in a heartbeat."

"Nah, a deal's a deal. I won't back out now or fuck him over. It's all good, don't you worry. I've given my word, and once I do that, whatever went on before is swept under the carpet, know what I mean?"

"I hope that is true. Because I do not mind killing you if you step out of line." Bart pulled up to the kerb where the SUV had been parked last night.

Now it was daylight, Moon got a better gander at the surroundings. This track, for want of a better description, ran down the rear of the backstreet where the base house stood on his left. Another structure, empty flats or apartments, had windows that weren't the gateway to any soul. All appeared blacked out; was the building derelict? Considering the state of the base house, this whole area might be about to go under reconstruction. Did anyone else even live around here? Or was that why Hendrik had chosen this area—because no one would hear gunshots or screams for help?

"Come on." Bart got out and strutted down the alleyway.

Moon took his main phone out as he exited the vehicle. He brought his screen to life. He'd already written a message earlier saying AT THE HOUSE, he just hadn't sent it, but he did now. He'd put a TRACK MY FRIEND app on his phone and shared it with the twins.

Bart disappeared from the alley, and Moon quickly sent a location pin just to be doubly sure. Messages deleted and phone returned to his pocket, he walked halfway down the alley and crouched, making out he tied his laces to account for why he was taking so long. Just as he knew he would, Bart popped his head round the side of the building, frowning. Moon glanced up, smiled, then went after him.

They walked into the house, Crabby Cunt standing guard, as if on hand to shoot Moon's brains out if he put a foot wrong.

"Afternoon," Moon said, giving him a wink. "No need for the weapon, is there? We're all friends here."

The bloke stared at him. Moon shrugged and trailed after Bart into the room with the table. Hendrik sat in his usual spot, this time, two cut-crystal glasses and a full bottle of amber alcohol in attendance.

"Have a seat." Hendrik reached for the bottle and made a song and dance about opening it, the *scritch* sound of the seal breaking a point he was making—that the booze hadn't been tampered with.

That didn't mean fuck all, though. Anyone could have injected something into the lid with a super-fine needle. Still, the fact Hendrik's glass was empty was a good sign, he didn't have a non-drugged drink in there. Moon wouldn't sip until the Dutchman had, though. Best to be careful an' all that.

Hendrik poured. "I trust you slept better at the hotel."

It was either a reminder that Hendrik had given Moon a lumpy mattress upstairs or Hendrik was testing whether he had a conscience about killing Ineke.

"Like a baby," he said, "although why that's a saying, I don't know. Babies don't sleep much at first, do they. Up all hours. Anyway, I slept fine, thanks. You?"

"I had a troubled night, unfortunately. One, we have a body we cannot locate—it just annoys me, not knowing everything—and two, my driver proved he cannot be trusted, so we had to deal with him."

Moon could have dropped Bart right in the shit for spilling secrets by saying he'd already told him, but he wasn't in the mood to fuck about. "Oh. Not good."

"No. But let's drink to our allegiance again, then go and see the women." Hendrik took a large gulp then opened his cigarette case. "Please, feel free to smoke." He lit his fag and closed his eyes briefly, staring at Moon through the grey cloud he exhaled.

The few puffs on the cigar Moon had indulged in on his way to get Ineke's breakfast had been heaven, and he grabbed the chance to have another few now. He smoked and drank—scotch—and if he was any good at pretending to be elsewhere, he could almost imagine he was at home if this place wasn't such a shithole.

Hendrik prattled on about the terms of the deal and how the chosen women would go back with Moon at first, then a second lot would be sent over with men escorting them, then a third and so on. Moon nodded and *ahhed* every so often, his mind half on the bloke's words and half on those that circled inside his head.

Crabby's still in the hallway.
There's Bart and Hendrik.
Three others are standing by the wall.
All present and correct.
Or are there more who I haven't met yet?

A pause came in Hendrik's boring drone, so Moon jumped in. "So, are you going to expand your workforce now you're branching out?"

"What do you mean?"

"You have six men now the driver's been sorted. Won't you need more if your empire's going to get bigger?"

"Six is enough for now."

Cheers for the confirmation. "Right."

Hendrik eyed him through the foggy smoke. "How many do *you* have?"

"Hundreds."

An eyebrow rose. "Why do you need so many?"

Why do you think, dickhead? "I've got my two most trusted, but then there's the coppers, the men on the street, the young lads who're my eyes and ears. Then you've got the fellas who collect protection money, the accountant, the people who work in the legit businesses I own—and the ones that aren't legit. No leader in London can run it by themselves. Yeah, they're the king or queen of their manor, so to speak, but it takes an army."

"I will do the same."

"I mean, what do you do to cover for what you're *really* doing? What law-abiding business do you run? I never did find that out."

"I don't."

"I had my men look into you before I took up your invitation to come over here the first time. Various sources say you're a CEO, but it doesn't state anything else."

"I am a CEO on paper." Hendrik smirked as if he had it all worked out.

He's got so much to learn, although I'll give it to him, he certainly made me think he's a hotshot. I believed the conniving bastard.

This was a lesson to Moon. Never take people as gospel. He'd let his guard down on this, took everything at face value, and maybe some of his arrogance had played a part there—he hadn't thought anyone would dare to fuck him over, incarcerate him in a room. "I see. Want my advice?"

Hendrik narrowed his eyes as though he hated *needing* the advice, but it was obvious he did. "Okay."

"Set up a proper front. That way, you're covered for the taxman and if the police come sniffing round your arse."

Hendrik cleared his throat. "I will look into it."

No, you won't. You'll be dead soon. "I've got a proposition for you, something that will expand your coffers even more. Interested?"

"Depends what it is." Hendrik poured then downed another shot like the booze was going out of fashion. Was he nervous? Did he have something up his sleeve, anxious about how it would play out?

"Two London leaders arrived here this morning. Good friends of mine. They came when I told them about the lucrative deal me and you made. They want in."

"Who are they?"

"The Brothers."

Hendrik's eyes lit up. "The Wilkes twins?"

"Yeah."

A nod. "I will speak with them, but I wish you had asked me first before you spoke about my business."

"But it's *my* business now, too, and as I'm running things at my end, I have the right to employ whoever I need to in order to make it work. The twins happen to have a lot of people on their books who I can use," Moon lied. "For me to poach their staff, I had to explain myself. They wouldn't have let me have any of their employees if I didn't, and you want me to start work with the women straight away, so…"

"Right. I understand. Where are they now?"

"At the hotel."

"Message them. Get them here."

Moon didn't bother taking umbrage at the bloke's tone, it wouldn't get him anywhere. He took his own phone out and tapped in a text. Pressed SEND. "Sorted."

Bart stepped over to snatch the phone. He stared at the screen.

Thank fuck I deleted the other message and location pin. "What's the matter?"

"Just checking." Bart handed the mobile back.

If he'd had to check, it meant they hadn't put a bug app on it, but then again, this could all be for show. Still, it didn't matter, not since Hendrik knew the twins were on their way. This lot would be stupid to hurt Moon now if that was their intention. Or maybe they were waiting for George and Greg to arrive so they could kill them, too.

Not knowing the gameplay did a number on Moon's nerves. He took turns puffing on his cigar and swigging scotch.

"Come, I want to show you something." Hendrik rose.

Moon stubbed his cigar out and slid it in his jacket pocket, glad the booze wasn't doing anything to him other than giving the usual buzz. "I'm all eyes."

Chapter Eleven

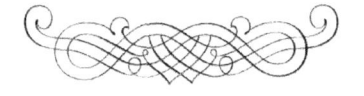

Hendrik resented Moon bringing the Wilkes men into this without his permission. Like he'd said, he wished he'd asked, but like *Moon* had said, this was also *his* business now. Unsettled by how quickly events could spiral out of his control, and that he'd been stupid to imagine he *could* control Moon once he was back in London—*I'm so naïve*—Hendrik promised himself some alone time later to go through all of his tumultuous thoughts. He'd walked into this new life without much planning, and it had become clear that he had a hell of a lot to think about. Not only did he have this to deal with but something else, too—another person controlling him, which pissed him off. He couldn't say no to them, though. They had him by the balls.

His knee-jerk reaction to hold Moon in that upstairs room had perhaps been rash, a childish decision, a petulant need to save face in front of his men. What he should have done was make an ally out of Moon like he had during the first visit, picked his brains over time, learned all he could about this kind of life, and put the refusal down to Moon having the right to choose whether he jumped on board. Instead, Hendrik's need to establish dominance and power had overtaken him.

It was one thing to act the gangster but another to do it with finesse. And he'd failed on the latter. He should teach himself how to play the long game—or get Moon to guide him.

Moon talking about Hendrik getting more of a workforce on the books, plus opening a legitimate business... It had rankled. Not only because someone more experienced than him had offered advice—but that it had been obvious Moon had needed to. The man had spotted a crack in Hendrik's castle and had stepped in to point it out—basically saying he was more superior and Hendrik might *think* he'd got his shit together but he hadn't. Moon was a dangerous person, and the only way Hendrik had been able to show him he meant business was to lock him in that room.

During their chat just now, inside his slowly withering-with-lack-of-confidence self, Henrik had been reduced to the young person he'd once been, the one he wanted to distance himself from, and it still smarted even now on the way down to the basement. He verged on slipping into the type of melancholy that had ruled his days before he'd pulled up his bootstraps and done something about his shitty life.

No, don't let this bring you back down.

Maybe he could sweep his faux pas out of his head by showing Moon the two men hanging from the ceiling prior to visiting the women. Dead bodies were a good way if getting your point across, and seeing them would boost Hendrik's ego. *He'd* ordered for them to be killed.

Him. He was *someone*. His men had obeyed him without question.

"Do you keep the women down here, then?" Moon asked behind him.

"Yes."

"Have they been here all this time, the same amount of time as me when I was in that room?"

"Yes." Hendrik smirked; he loved knowing something Moon hadn't. *Back in control.* He fist-bumped the air by his side, a thrill going through him. He could do this, be a big man, someone to be feared. So many people around here had fallen for his persuasive charm, as had the women who were greedy for a life abroad—*and* Moon, a supposed hard bastard who didn't let anyone pull the wool over his eyes.

Hendrik had created the illusion he was on a par with him, yet the veil had slipped somewhere along the line if Moon had highlighted his shortcomings. It grated, and Hendrik grew annoyed with himself that he hadn't successfully held off the self-flagellation until later. That was the problem with people like him, like Joep. The feelings associated with insecurity, of being brought up the way they had been, never left them. He wished there was a pill to erase the past and all the emotions associated with it.

He paused at the door and turned to Moon in the poor light from the bare, dusty bulb. "How do you forgive yourself for your mistakes?" Why had he said that? The words had emerged before he'd had a chance to think. They were supposed to remain as thoughts. But Maybe Moon, who'd already given him some good advice, would offer more.

"That's a difficult one," Moon said. "I still struggle from time to time to get over certain things, and just when you think you've got a handle on it, when you haven't thought about it for years, it pops back up to remind you."

Hendrik let out a sigh of irritation. Moon had been too honest—Hendrik had wanted a proper solution, not to be told he'd be plagued with thoughts of his awful upbringing forevermore, the poverty, the hunger, people looking at him like shit on their shoe. "So you do not have a technique to prevent you from going over and over your mistakes?"

"Well, killing people helps, although I don't do that much anymore. I've got men for that. But I watch, get satisfaction from teaching people their lack of respect pissed me off."

Was that a warning? From Googling, Hendrik had discovered that Moon was revered on his Estate, and because of him being an older man, Hendrik had perhaps made the mistake of thinking he would be easily cowed and manipulated. The two refusals had proved he wasn't, but after a stint in that room, Moon had capitulated in the end, he'd agreed to run the women. But what if he didn't? What if he let them go? What if strangling Ineke was just par for the course? What if it didn't bother him that Hendrik now had a picture of him in a bed beside a corpse?

What if those twins aren't here for a business deal?

A cold sluice of fear whipped through him. Had he made an error in choosing Moon? No, what he had to show him now would tell the man he wasn't to be messed with.

"Why?" Moon asked. "Are you struggling to be who you want to be because who you were has come knocking?" He laughed, although it wasn't unkind. "Happens to the best of us. We're learning every day, aren't we? About ourselves, our business, and other people. What we have to remind ourselves is that *we're* the top dog, and what *we* decide is what's going to happen."

He'd used the royal we, but what if he was really saying *I*? What if he was about to do something to Hendrik to prove *he* was the one in charge?

Utterly annoyed that he still wasn't truly confident in himself, Hendrik plastered on a smile that said otherwise. "Yes, we are the top dogs in our respective areas on the planet, and when we are in the other's domain, we have to bow to the rules." *You have to do what I say when you're in Amsterdam.*

Moon nodded. "Too right, which is why I had my change of heart. I forgot I wasn't in London but on *your* turf, and I can only apologise for any disrespect. But I will tell you, for future reference, that just because *you* want something to happen on someone *else's* turf, it doesn't mean it has to."

Another lesson in how these things worked. Far from wanting to bark at Moon and tell him not to threaten him, which he felt he had, Hendrik conceded that he'd do well to take any guidance offered. He was relatively new to this game, and his lack of practise showed. "Thank you for the reminder. I suppose I should apologise as well for expecting you to do what I want in London when it is up to you what happens on your Estate."

"All forgotten. So, the women?"

"I want you to see something else first." Hendrik pushed the door open and stared at Bart and two other men, still on the stairs, his glance telling them he had this from here.

Bart shook his head but slunk off regardless, likely muttering to himself that he didn't trust Moon with the boss. The others followed.

Moon peered inside the room then laughed so hard he bent over for a moment. He stood upright. "Fuck me, look at the state of his *face*!"

Hendrik studied Joep. The exposed flesh had hardened overnight, forming a hard crust. He hung from a rope attached to a large silver meat hook, and beside him, the driver, Daan, the scruffy, skinny prick who'd broken the rules. All Hendrik had wanted to do was give Daan a chance, to get him out of the life he'd lived, and this was how he'd repaid him.

"What do you think I should do regarding the way I run things?" Hendrik gestured for Moon to go into the room with him.

"What do you mean?" Moon stepped inside.

Hendrik closed the door. "I'm going to speak quietly so no one overhears should they come down, but I think I've made a colossal mistake."

"How come?"

Hendrik explained about all of his men having keys to the women's door. Moon's brow furrowed, and he folded both lips in over his teeth, contemplating.

"For a start, only you should have a key. Keep a spare elsewhere. *You're* the boss, your men aren't your equals and should never be made to think they are. Think of a triangle. You're at the top point. No one else should stand up there with you."

Hendrik nodded.

"That's how mistakes happen, see. Daan thought he could do whatever he liked. Probably thought, you know, they're prostitutes, so it wouldn't matter if he had a sample. The key gave him the impression he had carte blanche. But he was wrong—it's *your* choice whether he had the privilege, d'you get me?"

"Hmm. Thank you."

The viewing of Joep and Daan hadn't had the desired effect. Moon wasn't bothered by their presence or the state of them, and again, Hendrik realised he'd made a mistake. He'd asked for advice, so to then follow it up with a threat that death would happen to Moon if he failed to behave, well, it was stupid, wasn't it?

"Do you want my honest opinion?" Moon asked.

"Yes."

"You might not like it, so then you'd have to tell me I'll end up hanging beside these two pricks because I've overstepped the mark."

"I won't."

"But you planned to, didn't you."

"I did."

"Thought so. You're young, you're going to make wrong judgements, but the advice on offer is that there's always someone out there smarter than you, one step ahead, and you must never forget it. Don't become complacent like I did."

Hendrik smiled. Moon was referring to being locked in that room? Underestimating Hendrik?

"Like I said, we're all learning every day." Moon gave the dead men the once-over, chuckled, then sniffed. "The women?"

Hendrik filed away another subject to inspect later when he was alone—whether Moon was sincere or not. He led the way to the other room, slid the key in the lock, and turned it.

"Wait," Moon said. "Tell me what you were about to do."

"Go in and show them to you."

"Think. There are twelve of them. You've sent your men away. There's only you and me. Twelve women—they could overpower us, one of them could get your gun."

Feeling stupid, a novice, Hendrik took his weapon from the holster hidden beneath his suit jacket. "Stay back," he shouted towards the door. "Anyone moves, you get shot, and your bodies will be dumped on your parents' doorsteps."

He hadn't spoken to them in Dutch because he'd wanted Moon to understand what he'd said.

Moon patted him on the back. "That's better, son. But before you go in, what have you been doing to stop yourself being caught trafficking, as in, one of those parents reporting their daughters are missing? What safety measures are in place to prevent that?"

"We message their families from their phones every day to maintain the illusion they're happy to be going to England."

"Good. So all of them have families who think they're leaving for a better life?"

"Yes."

"All of them have people who care?"

"Yes."

Moon nodded slowly. "Another snippet. Next time, choose people who've got no one who gives a shit about them. Doing it your way means I'm going to have to keep up the pretence and message their people once or twice a week for God knows how long in London. It's a pest when I'm so busy, and the same will go for you with the next batch. You don't want to make extra work for yourself."

Hendrik could have cursed himself. He'd been too eager to secure the women, selecting whoever was the prettiest when they'd stood in front of their sex windows. He should have thought more. From now on, he'd up his game. Stop being so bull at a gate.

"Will you teach me? All…this. Everything?"

"Yeah." Moon flicked a hand towards the door. "Shall we go in, then? The twins will be here soon. You'll learn a thing or two from them an' all about how to play this game."

Moon grinned to himself behind Hendrik's back. The man was a fucking prat, and Moon's not-so-subtle threats seemed to have gone over his head. Why had Moon ever been scared in this house? In that room? Of Hendrik? It was so clear now that he shouldn't have been. The *façade* was what had scared him, what he'd *thought* he'd stumbled into—a bossman who'd kill him in an instant, what with those two blokes hanging in that room as evidence of his murder-happy temper, but deep down, Hendrik was floundering. Or was it because the twins were here, reminding Moon of who he was, that had given him the confidence to know Hendrik wasn't anyone to fear?

Whatever, Moon had dropped the ball, allowed himself to let that fear creep in during the long hours he'd spent alone with his thoughts. Prior to coming here he'd got above himself, thinking no one could take him down, when all of Hendrik's men had guns and could easily have shot him in the head. But it was just surface fluff, this outfit was nothing more than a sham led by a gutter rat in prince's clothing.

Either way, now Moon held all the cards, he could act accordingly. So he smiled, walked up and down the bottom of the beds and inspected each woman while Hendrik observed him for a reaction.

"I'll take them all," Moon said. He smiled at them in turn. "You're safe with me, girls, I promise."

Chapter Twelve

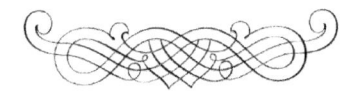

The hair had been styled, the nails polished, the trim completed. Dorothea put some rock music on in the living room, coming into the kitchen where Ineke did her homework at the island. Dorothea prepared herself a drink, taking vodka from the kitchen cupboard, pouring some out into one of Moeder's special glasses, right to the top, then adding water to the bottle from the tap. Why did she do that? So

Moeder wouldn't notice any had been taken? Dorothea sipped, closing her eyes. Moeder's dressing gown swung around the old woman's legs, the scent of perfume wafting from where it had embedded in the fibres.

Dorothea stopped and stared at nothing, as if a thought had come to mind. She glanced at her empty backpack on the floor, nodded, and put the glass down. She got on her knees, her bones creaking, and rooted about in the front pouch, bringing something out in a closed fist.

"Let's see what she makes of this *then. I'll show her. Fucking whore."*

Dorothea managed to get up without struggling too much and stomped out.

Ineke waited for a little while, then followed.

She found her upstairs in Moeder's bedroom, pressing something onto the lamp beside the bed. The base, a sparkly mass of small fake crystals, shone from the light beaming beneath the pleated cream shade. Ineke stood on the landing but moved to the side, poking half of her head around the jamb so she could dip out of the way if Dorothea turned around.

"That should do it," the old bitch said. "You can't even tell the difference."

Ineke ran into her bedroom, pretending to get another schoolbook. Just in time, too. The thud of the vile woman's footsteps bonked along the landing.

"What are you doing up here?" Dorothea asked.

Ineke spun round and held up her book. "I needed this."

Dorothea studied her, head cocked. "Hmm, get your backside into the kitchen."

Ineke scuttled past her and took the stairs as if Dorothea chased her, but when she got to the bottom and looked up, the horrible woman stood at the top.

"Go and see if my clothes are dry."

Ineke did as she was told and folded the laundry, taking the pile up to Dorothea who'd remained in place all that time, the weirdo. She grabbed the pile and swanned off into the bathroom to get dressed. Ineke once again went downstairs and got on with her homework.

It wasn't long before Dorothea appeared. She stuffed the rest of the washing into her backpack and zipped it up. Stood. Gulped some vodka until only half remained.

"Your mother is a wicked, wicked woman."

Yes, I know.

"She thinks she's so clever, but people are talking. They know."

Know what?

"*I mean, who in their right mind would go out as themselves when they're someone in her position?*"

Who else is she supposed to go as?

Ineke frowned. Sometimes, Dorothea talked in riddles.

"*You'd think she'd at least wear a wig or something, but no, she thinks she's untouchable, that she can do what the hell she likes. Well, I've had enough of this babysitting shit, all of her rules, and I'm not doing it anymore. This might well be the last time I look after you, kid.*"

She didn't really do that, it was Ineke looking after her with the 'pamper' sessions, but what was the point in saying anything?

"*Anyway, you're old enough now to look after yourself. I was on my own at twelve, so I don't see why you can't be. I'm going to bring her down. Prove to her she isn't in control. She's had stuff hanging over my head for too long, but it stops now.*" *Dorothea finished the vodka.* "*Wash the glass.*"

Ineke got up and did that, drying it, too. Dorothea put it and the bottle away, and it was as if a drink had never been stolen.

"*She'll roll in later with a man and won't even notice I've had my hair done. That's how drunk she gets. It'll all be out in the open after that, you'll see. People are already talking, her colleagues from the court. They think she's disgusting, so I heard, and she may as well have signed her own walking papers, because for a judge to fuck about with the men she's presided over in court, well…"*

Ineke digested that. Dorothea must be talking about the boyfriends Moeder brought home, those unseen, unheard men that Ineke wouldn't have known existed, except Moeder told her about them the next day.

"Do you like your father?"

Ineke wasn't sure how to answer that. She neither liked nor disliked him. She did wish he was nicer and that he'd take her away from all this. He confused her, as did Moeder and Dorothea, and she'd never understand any of them.

"Why?" Ineke asked.

"Because you'll be going to live with him soon."

"Why?"

"Because your mother is going to lose her job, this house. If she's not sent to prison, she won't be able to afford to live here because I'm going to expose her for the scam she's running — letting people off with lighter sentences, getting paid for it. And with all that crap she gets up to on Friday nights, she's not fit to have you in her custody. Other kids have been taken away

from their mothers for less, I should know. I haven't seen my daughter for forty years."

A wave of fear squeezed Ineke. Vader wouldn't want her, he'd already said, so she was destined for that cupboard, starvation.

"Anyway." Dorothea gestured to the homework. "Get that done then go to bed." She walked out. The music switched off, then came the sound of voices from the TV. Dorothea would park herself on the sofa for the rest of the night now.

Ineke finished what she had to do, packed her books away, and put her schoolbag in the cupboard. She passed the living room, where Dorothea slept in the dark, the flickers from the television pasting her face different colours. Ineke crept into Moeder's bedroom and stared at the lamp base, in the place where Dorothea's thumb had been pressing. One crystal was slightly bigger than the others, sitting on top of the one beneath. It had a tiny black dot in the middle. If Ineke hadn't known to look, she would never have spotted the difference. Would Moeder?

Dorothea's words pattered through her head. Whatever this new crystal was for, it meant Moeder wouldn't have a job anymore. Ineke sat on the bed, and she thought about what would happen to her if Moeder lost everything. Surely the starvation cupboard was one of Monster's cruel stories. Vader wouldn't really let her go there, would he? Greet, would she stop that from happening? Would she tell Vader to let Ineke live with them?

It was a chance Ineke was willing to take, so she stood, left the crystal where it was, and smoothed the quilt so Moeder wouldn't know she'd sat there.

Then she went to bed.

The following week when Dorothea arrived, she stopped Moeder from flouncing out and slamming the door. "Wait. There's something you need to see before you go."

Ineke watched from her perch at the island, seeing straight into the foyer.

Moeder (because she wasn't any of her personalities tonight; she'd complained the vodka didn't seem as strong, so she wasn't drunk), stared down at Dorothea's ancient hand on her arm. "Don't touch me, you filthy piece of shit. What have I told you about that? Have you forgotten the rules?" She flicked the hand away.

Dorothea smiled, revealing her gross, broken teeth, their tops brown. "Rules? We're playing by mine now."

"Excuse me? Has it slipped your mind what I did for you? You wouldn't be free if it wasn't for me. I saved you from years behind bars. Years."

"That story is boring now, and I've more than paid you back for it with all this free babysitting." Dorothea jerked a thumb over her shoulder. "You need to watch a little film." She took something from her backpack and waved it around.

A silver disc.

Moeder's faced paled, a touch of a Monster expression flickering around her eyes. "What is this nonsense?"

"You'll soon see." Dorothea trundled into the living room.

Moeder glanced at Ineke and pointed. "Stay there. Do not move."

Ineke stayed where she was until Moeder's laughter trilled. She tiptoed to the living room door and looked round it. Moeder and Dorothea stood with their backs to her , a slice of the TV between them. Moeder hadn't laughed with Dorothea, she'd laughed on the screen.

"Get on the bed," Moeder said.

It took Ineke a second to realise the voice had come from the speaker. She stared at the section in view, someone naked standing in front of the crystal, the bum thick with black hairs. Then whoever it was got on the bed. A hand trailed down the skin, Moeder's, her diamond ring visible, then her painted nails. Someone grunted, and she laughed again.

"What the fuck is this?" Moeder said, the real-life Moeder who stared to the side at Dorothea, her mouth trembling.

"I see you're shitting yourself." Dorothea smiled. "As you saw when you two went into the room, it's clear who you are. Let me rewind to refresh your memory."

"I don't need to see it again."

"But I want *you to see it. I'm in charge now." Dorothea used the DVD remote, and the screen was a series of flickering images in reverse.*

The footage stopped, then it resumed, showing Moeder entering her bedroom in the dress she'd gone out in last Friday night, followed by a young man in casual clothes. He didn't look like Vader, someone who had money and took care of himself, but more like a man you'd pass on the street, a nobody.

"Sem Faber," Dorothea said. "An associate of mine. Did you not wonder why he paid you so much

attention that night? Why he had to go home with you?"

"You fucking bitch," Moeder muttered.

"Certain people would like to get hold of this, wouldn't they?"

"You wouldn't dare."

"Oh, I think I would." Dorothea switched the TV off. "So, this is what's going to happen. You're not going to ask me to come to this house ever again and look after your weird daughter. You're going to pay me thirty thousand to keep my mouth shut, and you're also going to give me ten for Sem. If you do, no one will see this footage—we have copies—but if you don't, say goodbye to your life as you know it."

That didn't make sense. Dorothea had told Ineke she was going to expose her. So was this a trick? Get the money then tell everyone anyway?

"That's bribery," Moeder seethed.

"No different to what you've been doing to me all this time, and God knows how many others. All those men you bring back here, they're bad boys, they've stood in the stand while you've given them short sentences, and when they get out of prison, you hunt them down and use them for sex to repay you for your 'kindness'. What are you, a sex maniac? People know. They're talking. Your reputation's on the verge of

being in tatters. I'd stop if I were you. Or be more discreet."

"Get out of my house."

"Oh, I will, but I'll be back this time next week to collect." Dorothea tilted her head at Moeder. "From one woman to another, if you're fucking as many men as you are, it's obvious you're looking for something you can't find. I heard therapy will sort that out—or maybe you should get over your ex-husband and move the fuck on."

She turned towards the door, her attention on the floor. Moeder snatched up a brass figurine and raised it, going after her, face contorted.

"I wouldn't," Dorothea said. "Sem knows to phone the police if I don't check in with him tonight."

Moeder lowered the ornament. Dorothea smiled and walked on.

Ineke ran back to the island and picked up her pen. Bent her head so it appeared she was busy. The front door slammed in Moeder fashion, but the woman herself hadn't left. She came storming into the kitchen, grabbed a fresh bottle of vodka from the cupboard, and twisted the lid off. She gulped down the liquid that would turn her into Monster, but for now, the anger she'd displayed with Dorothea had gone, replaced by a Verdrietig wail.

"Oh God, oh God, what am I going to do?" She sank to the floor, her back against a base unit, and swigged more drink. *"I'm finished. That amount of money, it's too much."* She glared at Ineke. *"Go to bed before I kill you. Go. Now!"*

Ineke scrambled from her stool, indecisive as to whether she should put her homework away—she wasn't allowed to leave it out—but Verdrietig, or whoever the hell Moeder was, had said now, *so she should run, shouldn't she?*

So Ineke ran.

Life had been a case of keeping quiet for Ineke during the week after Dorothea had produced the silver disc. Moeder had alternated between being Verdrietig and Nors, crying one minute, grumpy the next. She spent a lot of time whispering to someone on the phone, a phone Ineke hadn't seen before, saying if they didn't help her and they found out she'd let them off a long sentence, there might be a retrial and he'd end up in prison to serve proper time.

"I don't know what evidence she has apart from the DVD," Nors had said. *"We can't risk not doing anything."* A pause where she'd listened. *"No, if I had*

that amount of money to hand I might have paid her off, but I don't. My assets are tied up in stocks and shares, so I have limited funds. What? Of course I'd pay you! How? Once a month in cash. I can't withdraw it all at once, not when the police will be sniffing around. They might need to speak to me. God knows how many people she's told that she babysits for me."

Ineke kept herself as small as possible, but maybe she needn't have bothered. Moeder was in her own world, acting as if she didn't even have a child, and she'd gone to work with grey patches beneath her eyes where she hadn't slept much. Ineke had listened to her pacing in the middle of the night, her cries, her shouts of anger. Each morning, she expected to find her dead, an empty pill packet by her side, Verdrietig gaining the upper hand and fully taking her over, whisking her to Heaven, or maybe that would be Hell.

Those pills. She'd told Vader and Ineke she no longer took them, but men came to the door sometimes, handing padded envelopes over. Did they contain the medication? Moeder always gave them an envelope in return, so did that have money in it? Why didn't she go to the pharmacy and collect them? Maybe she didn't want anyone to know she was secretly back on the drugs that had helped her through the depression after

Ineke was born. Moeder was so secretive, so desperate to put on a front, that it would make sense for her to have them delivered.

She kept the pills in the back of her wardrobe, in the cubed sides that held her shoes. Ineke had found them one day when she'd looked for a pair of high heels. She'd played dress-up while Moeder had gone out one afternoon. They troubled her, those pills, because many of the packets were full. Was she saving them to take all at once, like Verdrietig had promised she would one day? Or was the knife, also with the bottle, be what she would use?

"You did what?" Moeder had whispered into the phone on Thursday night. "How could you be so stupid? They'll be found! I expressly asked for that not to happen. What do you mean, blood? For God's sake, did you stab them?" A long space of silence. "I suppose that makes sense. The water will wash any evidence away. Okay, but what about a motive? Why would they have been stabbed? She was what*? And you didn't think to tell me? I've spent most of this week worrying about everything, and had I known this, I wouldn't have cared—I'd have had something on* her. *So it'll now look like her and this Sem were the targets of a drug dealer. Right. Fine."*

Saturday had crawled round again, and Dorothea hadn't come to collect. Moeder hadn't gone out last night, and she'd nipped to the supermarket not long ago. As Ineke had finished her chores, she went into the living room to watch television. She switched it on. Moeder had been obsessively following the news this week, and Ineke wanted to know why. She selected the right channel and sat, staring at the red ticker tape at the bottom of the screen: WOMAN FOUND DEAD IN CANAL. *The scene showed police in white suits near one of the bridges, talking amongst themselves. The camera panned. People had stopped to stare behind a cordon, then the camera moved again, landing on a lady in a blue coat holding a microphone.*

"Last night, the body of a woman was taken out of the canal. Dorothea van de Vuurst, sixty-five, was from Slotervaart. She had been missing since last Saturday night."

Panicked, Ineke stared at the screen, her heart hurting where it beat so fast. How had she died? Had she fallen into the canal and drowned? And why was she missing? Where had she gone?

"She had been stabbed repeatedly."

No. No! Nors had said about a stabbing on the phone.

"Her neighbour, Sem Faber, is still missing," Blue Coat continued. *"Police believe the two are connected as they were last seen together at nine p.m. on Saturday."*

A picture of a man flashed up. He was about twenty — Ineke guessed that because of how her teacher looked, and she'd said she was twenty-five, but this man was a bit younger. Dark hair —

the bum thick with black hairs

— and brown eyes, the beginnings of a beard. Dorothea had wanted money for him, he was the man on the video in Moeder's room, and with him missing and Dorothea dead, those phone calls...

Had Monster sent someone after them? Was that why Verdrietig had cried last night about getting caught? It hadn't made any sense then, but it did now. A cold clutch of fear gripped Ineke, so much so she shook with it, and she worried about the police finding out Moeder had done something, coming here to arrest her. Who had Verdrietig been speaking to? Whoever it was must have hurt Dorothea. So where was Sem?

"If you've seen this man in the past five days, then contact the police who are extremely concerned regarding his mental state."

What did that mean? Had Sem killed Dorothea?

The screen returned to Blue Coat. "As you can see, the canal is being dredged as we speak, and all cruises have been suspended. Back to you in the studio, Dirk."

Dirk, an older man with grey hair, gave the camera a grim smile.

Ineke switched the TV off and ran to her room, her thoughts clashing. Verdrietig must have heard about the body in the canal last night, because she'd paced up and down, crying, pill packets lined up on the worktop.

"I'm going to take them all before I get caught. I can't face this. It's all your father's fault. If he hadn't left me, none of this would be happening." She'd glared at Ineke across the kitchen. "If you hadn't been born..."

Was this the end for Moeder? Was it time for the cupboard?

Chapter Thirteen

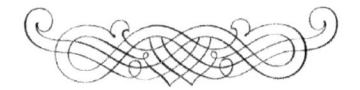

George didn't think much of Crabby Cunt who'd opened the door, his gun pointing at them. But it wasn't like he could do or say anything about the disrespect, was it. It was so alien being here, the lack of regard a hard pill to swallow when he was so used to people knowing who he was and doing as they were fucking told, doing what he *expected*. It brought home that he may well be a king in the East End, but he was a lowly subject here. It didn't sit right, as if something inside him itched, but he'd have to get over his entitled sense of self-importance—that's what it was, after all, and he was oddly glad he could admit it. Progress. He'd only be important here once deaths occurred, then Crabby would regret his scowl and lack of manners, his barked, "Who are you?" coming back to haunt him when the business end of his own gun was pressed to his head later on.

"George and Greg Wilkes. Hendrik is expecting us."

Crabby whistled between his teeth, an annoying command, one that spoke of *his* sense of self-importance. A weird-looking middle-aged bloke appeared at the end of the hallway. Tall, average build, with the air of Princess Diana's old butler about him, or maybe an accountant. Certainly no one to worry about visually, but Moon had already warned them that Bart, if this was who it was, had possible unknown depths, could perhaps be unpredictable.

"Bart," the butler-man said by way of introduction. "Hendrik is through here." He gestured behind him, a ring glinting on his thumb.

George brushed past Crabby and into the house, deliberately elbowing him in the gut. "Oh, sorry, I'm a bit of a clumsy bastard."

Crabby scowled, wafted his gun to encourage Greg to hurry up and get inside—another bit of rudeness—then shut the door. George glanced at his brother: *What an arrogant dick*. Was that how George came across to people? Probably. But wasn't it essential that he did, given his role in London? He excused his own behaviour based on that, but what excuse did Crabby have? He was just a foot soldier.

He'll get what's coming to him, so concentrate on the plan.

Greg skirted past and followed Bart. George took in the surroundings—stairs to the left, a door beneath them, maybe to the basement, the top a slant to accommodate the rise of the steps. A door to the right, closed. And another at the end. He tailed his twin through there to a room. A table, chairs, and men. Hendrik sitting opposite, Moon beside him. Bart now pressing his back to the wall beside the door. Greg. Three men in the corners, all with guns.

George made eye contact with Moon, who'd watched him scoping out the participants, and asked the silent question.

"It's just us and these six gentlemen," Moon said. "The prick driver was a naughty boy and sampled one of the women last night. He's dead. Hendrik doesn't fuck about. He won't stand for nonsense."

He's pretending he holds Hendrik in some kind of awe. Good.

"Bloody disgusting liberty." George eyed four crystal glasses on the table and a bottle of booze, then flicked his attention to Hendrik who hadn't done the gracious host bit and risen to shake their hand. *That's another black mark against you, sunshine.* "George Wilkes."

Hendrik finally stood. "Hendrik Alderliesten." He stuck his hand out, staring, eyes wide, a faint blush coating his cheeks—and a sheen of sweat.

What the fuck's up with him?

George reached over the table and shook it— quickly, in case the sweat extended to Hendrik's palm—then let it go. Greg stepped forward and introduced himself, appearing decidedly annoyed by the lack of etiquette around here.

Was *he* feeling the pinch of not being feared, too? The complete indifference to who they were?

We've got too used to the hype about us.

"We'll sit, shall we?" George stated, "seeing as you haven't offered."

Moon choked on laughter and turned it into a cough.

Hendrik bristled but hid it sharpish. "I apologise. I was a bit starstruck. I've heard many things about you. Please, take a seat. Drink?"

Starstruck? That's a bit more like it.

Although the belated respect didn't feel as good as it should. No amount of explanations from Hendrik would save his life now, so even though he'd come late to the welcome-the-leaders party and had at last remembered how to treat George and Greg, it wouldn't go in his favour.

"No, thanks." George sat. "I don't drink on the job."

Which is a lie, because I do indulge sometimes. I just don't trust you haven't doctored what's in those bottles, you slimy bastard.

Once Greg had taken a seat, George continued.

"So, what are your terms if we decide to help you out here?" He'd made it clear they would *choose*, they wouldn't be told. It undermined

Moon somewhat, showing up his weakness in not being stronger with Hendrik, but that couldn't be helped.

Hendrik poured drinks for himself and Moon and explained how he expected this to work, except he must have had a personality transplant, because he said, "Of course, I can't tell you what to do or how to behave in your own area of the world, so as long as I get a cut of the earnings sent to me via bank transfer once a week, that will be good enough."

Moon radiated smugness.

Ah, so they've had a chat, have they?

"And how are you going to explain a weekly transfer of thousands of pounds a week?" George asked. "I wouldn't use a bank. I'm fucked if I'll go down that route no matter how much money is involved. We have specific businesses, genuine ones, that can't be tainted—we won't risk us getting shopped for sending some bloke in Amsterdam money with no explanation as to what it's for. Our accountant wouldn't be happy."

"Shopped?"

"Arrested."

Hendrik pondered that. "I hadn't thought about the implications of that."

No, because you're a no-mark playing a big boy's game.

It was so weird. Hendrik looked the part, all suave and smooth, but he was far from being like them. If George hadn't spent the majority of his childhood in awe of Ron Cardigan, watching him, seeing how an Estate was run, he and Greg would have been like Hendrik when they'd first taken over. He shuddered at the thought.

"So it would have to be cash, collected in person by one of you lot," George said.

"That would mean sending my men to the UK weekly. There's air fares, expenses…"

George shrugged. "So? You must have a front that makes it look like you employ them legitimately. They could be coming over for that."

Moon lit a cigar. "Hendrik's still in the process of starting a legit business. These things take time."

In other words, he's been a dick and hasn't covered his arse yet. What a complete fanny. "Right, well, you'd better get it sorted quickly if you want us to take some girls on. How long will you need?

Our offer to help you out is only on the table for another couple of months."

Hendrik sat straighter. "You can always walk away, considering I didn't *choose* you. Moon told me you were interested."

If that was the only barb the bloke could think of, he was sorely lacking in the snark department.

Up your game, son. Get my anger going, for fuck's sake.

George glanced at Greg. "Shall we be off, then?"

Greg stood and straightened his suit jacket fronts. "Yeah, this isn't for us. If all the ducks aren't in a row, it's best we bow out." He smiled. "Nice to meet you, Mr Alderliesten. All the best."

Greg left first, and George trailed after him, stepping over the threshold into the hallway. No one called them back, which was a good thing. George turned, gave them all a nod as if to say he understood they needed privacy to talk about whatever the fuck Hendrik wanted to talk about, and he closed the door. Greg had reached the other end of the hallway and stood staring at Crabby.

George approached the moody sod with the gun. "Hendrik said we can have a butcher's at the dead men."

"Butcher's?" Crabby's thick eyebrows met in the middle.

"A look. He said you had to take us down there."

Crabby sighed and marched towards the room they'd just been in. George held his breath, waiting for the game to be up, but Crabby stopped in front of the sloping door under the stairs and opened it. He went through the space, and George glanced at Greg.

"Fucking twunt," he whispered.

They followed him down the dark staircase, faint light at the bottom. Crabby entered a room, George and Greg going in after him. Two bodies dangled. Crabby held his gun out, as if he waited for them to do something so he could shoot them.

"What's up with this one's face?" George walked closer to the body. Closer to Crabby on his right.

"He had the boil."

"The boil? What, it was *that* big?"

"I do not understand."

"You know, a boil, dunno what you call it, but they often appear on your arse. They get a bit sore, and sometimes the doctor lances them."

Crabby shook his head in disdain. "No, not that. He had hot oil poured on him." His face held the type of expression that said he hoped *they'd* get the boil and he'd relish watching them burn.

"Oh, *that* kind of boil. Lovely." George leaned nearer to whisper, "Did *you* pour it? Did you enjoy hearing him scream?"

"No, that is Bart's job."

"What's yours, to stand there looking ugly?"

Crabby raised his weapon. George chuckled, punched the side of Crabby's forearm, and the quick, unexpected movement meant he dropped the gun. It skittered across the floor. George clamped a hand around Crabby's throat and walked him towards the wall. Pushed him up against it. Got right in his face.

"Now listen to me, you fuckwit. I didn't appreciate your lack of manners upstairs when we arrived. Where I come from, people are nice to us else they find themselves in our warehouse. Once they're in there, I tie them to a chair and torture the fuck out of them. Sometimes I cut them up with my circular saw while they're still alive. In the absence of my tools, I'll just have to use my hands. Strangle the fuck out of you like Moon was supposed to do to Ineke, except he didn't." He paused. "She's still alive."

Crabby raised his hands to claw at George's arm, his face turning purple. "Hendrik...will...kill you...for that."

"Nah, mate, *we'll* be killing *him*. He fucked with the wrong person. Moon's one of our best mates, so to hear he was kept upstairs, in a shitty little room, well, you can imagine how we feel about it."

Greg came to stand beside Crabby, inspecting the gun. "Silencer."

"It could still make a bit of a pop," George said. "I think I'll just go with my initial method."

"You said it takes too long and hurts your hands," Greg said.

"Yeah, well, maybe I want to see this wanker struggling to breathe. Sore hands will be worth it."

"Just let me cap him one in the side of the head," Greg said. "Or at least string him up like the other two. There's a spare meat hook in the ceiling."

All this time, George had been staring at his brother and squeezing Crabby's neck tighter so it looked like their captive was of no consequence. George switched his attention to the man currently wheezing, his attempts to prise George's grip off him ineffectual and slowing.

"Got a family, have you?" George asked.

A louder wheeze.

"Was that a yes? Then they're going to miss you, because you're not going home, my old son. Do it, Greg. You were right, my hand's aching, and anyway, I'm bored."

Greg raised the gun and pressed the muzzle to Crabby's temple. "Step back. You'll get blood on you. No forensic suits here."

George let go, moved out of the way, and Greg pulled the trigger. The sound of the gun's retort seemed a bit loud, so as Crabby fell to the floor, as blood and brain sprayed on the wall, George and Greg waited for the clatter of footsteps. But this room was at the front of the house, and the table room at the back, so maybe they'd be okay. Besides, Moon would likely be talking and laughing loudly, regaling them with stories about London, as per the plan. They might not have heard anything.

"Come on." George gave a crumpled-in-a-heap Crabby one last glance and walked upstairs. In the hallway, he paused, waiting for Greg. "I'll go in now and say there's a problem in the basement. Keep that gun out of sight." He tapped on the door, opened it, and poked his head round. "Sorry to disturb you, but that bloke who was at the front door told us to let you know there's an issue downstairs. We thought it best we stay in case you need us. He's already gone down there."

Hendrik shot from his seat, but Butler Bart got to the door first. Either he was leading the charge because he thought he was some kind of bully boy or he genuinely wanted to save his boss the trouble. Bart shot downstairs, gun held high in both hands—*what a fucking munter*—and Greg nipped after him. By the time Hendrik had got to George, the unmistakable pop of a suppressed gunshot gave the game away.

"What the fuck's going on? I reckon your bloke's turned rogue. Or did you tell him to do this?" George didn't wait for Hendrik's reply. He rushed down to the basement.

Footsteps thudded after him, so he didn't have much time. He found Greg in the room, a gun in each hand, Bart dead on the floor. Greg handed him Bart's gun and motioned with his head for George to stand in the corner hidden by the door.

"No idea how many bullets we have between us," Greg whispered.

A shadow passed the crack by the hinges, and George lifted the gun. Hendrik appeared in the room, and George fired. Hendrik staggered forward, his head whacking into one of the hanging bodies, then he slumped down on the flagstones, a pool of blood creeping onto his shirt over his heart. A flash of Greg being gunned down in that abattoir flounced through George's head, and he shoved it away.

Another shadow, and this time one of the blokes from the table room came in. Bullets flew, the man hitting the deck. One more shadow. He didn't pass the threshold, though, must have been staring in at the bodies on the floor.

George crept to the hinge gap, spotted him, aimed, and fired. "Fucking hell, help us, will you?" he shouted. "The bloke who let us in the house has lost his shit!"

"Shut up," Greg barked in a piss-poor Dutch accent.

"What's going on?" Moon called.

"Hang on," George said. "Get that other fella to come and speak to this one, will you? He doesn't seem to understand us. We've tried to talk to him, but all he's interested in is shooting fucking bullets. I've got a bastard gun aimed at my face."

"Sort it out, will you, Luuk?" Moon said.

One final shadow by the hinges, this Luuk fella. "Wat gebeurt er, Pieter?"

George didn't know what the chuff he'd said, except he'd said it to someone called Peter. Crabby, he assumed. "He's behind the door, so watch it."

Luuk stepped in, over the bodies, and peered round the door, meeting the end of George's gun. Luuk's eyes widened, and he tossed his weapon to the floor and slowly raised his hands. It was clear he was fine with standing in the table room looking menacing but that he didn't know how to follow it through. A momentary flicker of pity hit George in the chest—this was nothing but a lad, but he couldn't be trusted to keep his gob shut so had to be sorted.

"I do not want to die." Luuk's voice trembled, the poor bastard.

Bet he's wishing he didn't agree to work for Hendrik now. Or maybe he was forced. It's obvious this isn't his bag.

George locked his emotions behind a steel door in his head. "Shame, because you've got no choice, but first, I want to know if there's anyone who's likely to find you all. Come looking."

"No."

"Are you sure?"

"Yes. Please, I have a daughter, a wife…"

"Bully for you." George shot him in the forehead and didn't bother watching him fall — he couldn't stand the guilt. He turned round to Greg. "Sorted. But do you know what pisses me off?"

"What's that, bruv?"

"We haven't got gloves on. We'll have to wash the guns before leaving them down here."

"I didn't think of that," Moon said.

George could have said Moon hadn't thought of a lot of things lately, but he didn't bother. Rubbing salt in the wound now might be tolerated, but once they got back to London, Moon might want to teach him a little lesson. *Sod that.* "Let's get our arses in gear."

Greg dragged whoever was in the passageway into the room. George stepped out and stared at Moon on the stairs.

"The women are in there." Moon pointed to another closed door. "You'll have to get the key. All the men have got one."

"Fishing about in a dead man's pockets? Fuck's sake." George shook his head but got on with it. The quicker they left this place the better.

Chapter Fourteen

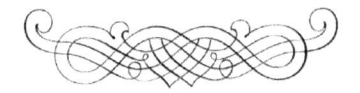

Moon entered the second basement room. All of the women stared at him, eyes wide. What a fucking pitiful sight, each on their beds, bunched up at the head end, hugging pillows or knees as though he was about to belt the shit out of them. They presented well, although his distaste for them having to put sexy underwear and makeup on still lingered from when he'd been in here with Hendrik not long ago. They'd been primped for his inspection.

"It's okay," he said, hands up to show he meant no harm. "Do you all speak English?"

A few nods came his way.

"I've got something to tell you, and it needs to be kept a secret, all right? I mean, I don't want to threaten you and traumatise you any more than you've already been, but I mean it, no one must say anything. For this to work, I need to be able to go back to London without any trouble."

He waited for them to stop staring over his shoulder at George. Greg had gone up to the office to root around for their passports and to see if he could find Ineke's phone.

"The men who held you here aren't going to be a problem for you any longer." He scanned the faces, gauging which woman had picked up on what he *hadn't* said. Blank canvasses, all but one.

"They are dead?" a blonde asked, her hair a satiny sheet around her shoulders.

"Yes." A nasty thought struck, and much as he didn't want to say it, he was going to have to. It would create trauma responses for months or years to come, maybe even nightmares, but in this world you had to save yourself if you dabbled in death, and he didn't intend to spend time in a Dutch prison over this bollocks. *God forgive me, girls, but…* "Except one. He's still out there, so if you breathe a word, who knows what he'll do."

Two women cried.

"What about the other men?"

"They're in the room down the hall. Now this is where the secret comes in. No police, understand? No one can know you were held here—we can't have the bodies being discovered yet. We need a few hours to get the place cleaned first."

"It's not like we can say anything to anyone anyway, is it," the blonde said. "You will be taking us to England and—"

"No, I won't. I told you you'd be safe with me, and you will."

"Why not keep us in here until you have cleaned?"

"Because I want to let you go as soon as possible, get you out of this shithole. I didn't want any part of this, but I was locked in a room like you until I agreed to do what Hendrik wanted. The only reason they released me was because I pretended I'd take you to the UK."

"Who is he?" Blonde asked, pointing at George.

"My friend. His brother's here, too, trying to find your passports. We're on your side, okay? You should go home, say nothing about this."

Shrieks of happiness erupted from a couple of them, but one or two eyed him funny, as if they thought he was lying. Not a surprise. Hendrik had pedalled them a good deal then reneged on it.

"I swear, I'm not mucking you about, you can go. Make up some story as to why you went home. Your phones might be found, too. Hendrik's men have been sending texts to your mums and dads or whatever. It's a fucked-up situation, but it's over now. Can I trust you to keep your mouths shut? Unless, of course, you want that other fella to come and find you."

Blonde nodded. "I just want to see my mother. I do not want to remember...this."

Moon grimaced. "What about everyone else? We're saving you, not treating you badly. Do I have your word you'll pretend this never happened? We've *killed* people for you, and we need to be able to go home, too. Let the bastards rot, they don't deserve proper funerals, and if the other bloke knows you haven't told on the gang, then he'll likely leave you alone."

"Hendrik said we would have a good life, but he lied," Blonde muttered.

"When something sounds too good to be true, it usually is. Don't ever trust anyone again when they promise you the world, all right?" Moon smiled. "Except me, because I'm not lying. Get dressed into something more appropriate. It's bloody cold out there, and you can't walk around in your undies. We can't risk being seen by cameras, so you'll have to make your own way. We'll wait upstairs while you get ready."

He turned and bumped into George, closing the door to give them some privacy.

"Reckon they'll keep schtum until we've gone home?" he whispered.

George tugged at his fake beard. "Who can tell, but I'm not prepared to kill them to keep them quiet. Good move by saying one of them is still out there, by the way. Wicked, but... As for any ramifications while we're still in Amsterdam, I'm in disguise, they wouldn't recognise me or Greg without this getup, but *you*, baldy..."

Moon strutted past him. "Enough of that baldy nonsense. I've got other things to worry about with my fingerprints being in this house. That room, the glasses I drank from…" He sensed George following.

"Maybe we should torch the house. It means the bodies being found sooner than we'd like, but if we're lucky, the SUV we hired won't have been caught coming here."

"No, I'd rather we clean it."

"*We*? Who do you think I am, Mrs Hinch?"

"Who?"

"That cleaner on social media."

"Hmm, if the caps fits…"

"Sod off."

Upstairs, Moon rooted around in the kitchen, intrigued to find a larder cupboard stocked with supplies. There was so much bleach it bothered him—how many blood spills had been mopped up in this place? What, exactly, had Hendrik been up to?

George came up behind him. "Rubber gloves. Bloody hell! I could have done with those earlier."

Moon tutted. "Shut up moaning. We'll stick the guns in a bucket of hot soapy water and scrub the buggers. Did you two touch anything in that room downstairs?"

"Only the driver's neck, but I closed the door of the meeting room."

"Then let's get to work. I bet it bites that your cleaning crew aren't here to save you the job."

"Fuck you."

In a flurry of desperation to get out of the house, the women had left, passports and phones in hand, their promises of keeping it quiet hushed and sounding sincere. Maybe Hendrik and his men had frightened them enough that they didn't dare to say otherwise—maybe they thought Moon, George, and Greg were just as bad as them, despite letting them go, and they feared for their lives.

Uneasy about them going out there and grassing to the police, regardless of those promises, Moon sighed. No matter how he felt, they had to clean this house—he couldn't risk his prints being found.

They might still be. What if we miss a bit?

With George and Greg busy with their sprays and cloths elsewhere, the paranoia and uncertainty of whether the police would arrive any second had Moon using his elbow to move objects in the cleaning cupboard.

"What the fuck's *that*?"

He took a pair of rubber gloves out of a packet and slid them on, putting the packet in his pocket because he'd touched it. Reaching towards the contraption, he pulled it out. It had a solid plastic base with an electrical cord and a transparent vessel half filled with water. Coming off that, a long slim hose with a white wand at the end. A power-washer. He crouched, tugged the stopper off the canister, and sniffed. Bleach.

Chuffed to bits he'd be able to douse his room from top to bottom then scrub with one of the hard-bristle brooms, plus drench the men's bodies, he got on with filling a bucket with bleach water so he could top the canister up. His suit would likely get fucked from splashes, but that was the least of his worries.

Chapter Fifteen

All of them still wearing pink rubber gloves, Greg, George, and Moon walked out of the house three hours later. The dead men's phones had been switched off—the blokes with families would be reported missing by tomorrow at the latest, and the last ping of a mast would indicate they'd been at the house, but it didn't matter. Greg didn't expect to still be here by then, but if they were, who could prove they'd come here and killed people? This area was abandoned, and he'd doctored the hired SUV's number plate with the black tape he'd brought with him in his suitcase, also taping up the little logo on the back that stated it was a rental car. If they'd been caught on CCTV, two bearded men would be looked for. He could only hope they got away with it. If not…

There was the slight issue of Moon sending the images of a 'dead' Ineke to Bart, Bart likely passing them on to Hendrik. Although he'd used the burner, Moon's face was visible. Even with the phones disposed of, which they would be at some point, the police could still contact the phone companies and maybe get those messages. It was such a pisser that they didn't have a copper to turn to who'd let them know whether the phones were burners or on contract. Mind you, all of them were the same as the one given to Moon, cheap efforts, so maybe they were throwaways without any names linked to them.

They'd just have to hope for the best on that.

Moon had insisted on power-washing and scrubbing every room, just in case; the bleach/water combination would do a number on any evidence, fucking things up for forensics because of everything being wet. George had used a steel-wire scouring pad on Hendrik's palm because he and Greg had shaken hands with him, then he'd poured neat bleach onto it. He'd looked a bit unhinged while doing it, and Greg had put it down to his brother needing to cause some damage, considering his usual torture tactics hadn't come into play here. Skin had peeled away by the time he'd finished, and he'd grinned.

All the while, Greg had expected a knock on the door—or worse, the police kicking it down, his nerves shot to pieces. He'd sometimes thought his anxiety levels in London had reached their peak, especially with George going out as a rebel in his Ruffian persona, but this, here, was on another level.

Now they'd stepped into the deserted street, he scanned the area for hiding officers who waited for them to emerge—paranoia was a bitch, but then was this self-preservation? The need to wrap this the fuck up and go home, where they were safer? Being out of his comfort zone didn't suit him. There was something to be said about running around the streets you knew, the familiar, as opposed to a foreign country.

When George had got the call from Debbie while they'd been with Ichabod in the Taj, Greg had felt bad for thinking it, but he hadn't wanted to come here and get Moon out of the shit. He hadn't voiced that, but his first thought was to keep George out of it, that Moon had made his own bed and should lie in it. Why should Greg's brother be dragged into it, especially when his mood swings—or alter swings—were unpredictable? Greg had groused to himself that Debbie should have asked Alien and Brickhouse to come here and get their boss, but of *course* she'd have turned to The Brothers, the two people who always had her back. But still…it had pissed him off.

Front door shut, they stood in the weird, stagnant silence, as if the buildings held their breaths along with them. A bird cawed, startling Moon, and Greg took it as an omen to get the fuck out of there. Halfway down the alley, he sucked in a breath. The buzz of a whiny engine had all three of them stopping.

"Shit," George whispered.

"Which end is it coming from?" Greg asked.

Moon cocked an ear. "The front."

George stared at the sky, clearly on the verge of blowing his top. "Then we don't need to worry about it. Our motor's in front of the SUV that was there when we arrived. If we sod off now, we won't be seen by whoever that is."

"Maybe I wasn't lying to the women," Moon said quietly. "Maybe there *is* someone left."

Greg walked back the way they'd come and surreptitiously peered around the edge of the building. A moped stood propped up at the cracked kerb, a dull black helmet hanging on one handle. He returned to George and Moon. "A bloke, well, a kid really, about nineteen. Got any euros on you?"

Moon fished in his wallet and produced a couple of hundred. "What are you up to? I swear to God, if this drags us into any shit when we're almost home and dry…"

"Go and get in the hire car and lie on the back seat," Greg said to Moon. To George, "Get in the driver's side and put your hood up."

"Fucking hell, bruv…*really*? Do we need to hang around, you doing whatever the fuck you're planning to do?"

"Yes."

"And I thought *I* was the reckless one."

Greg adjusted his glasses, catching an eyeful of pink rubber glove. "Think about it. We've got Hendrik's SUV we didn't factor in. It needs getting rid of, and *we* can't do it."

"Where are the keys?" George asked.

"In my pocket. I was going to leave them on the bonnet for some scummy cunt to nick the car, but this way is better." Greg took the cash and strutted round to the front door. He reckoned sounding Russian would be about right. "Vot are you doing here?"

The newcomer squinted. Looked at the gloves and frowned. "Coming to see Hendrik. Why do you need to know?"

Greg eyed him through the clear lenses of his thick-framed glasses. "He is out of country, flew to my homeland this mornink. I vill join him later where we vill meet and drink vot-ka. I haf job for you." He flapped the money, those fucking gloves a flashing beacon that he'd been up to no good or he was a weirdo with a pink rubber fetish. "You like these, eh?"

A blank stare.

"They are fashion accessory." Greg smiled, lips closed. "Everyone in my country wear them."

Another blank stare. A sigh. "Look, what do you want me to do?"

"I need you to take car to Hendrik's house. I borrowed it but forgot to ask where he lives." Greg took the keys he'd snatched from Bart's pocket out of his. "I haf friend here now who vill take me to airport. I haf no time for doing this." He put the keys and cash in the bloke's hand. "Thank you. Goodbye."

He stalked back towards the alley.

"Where's the car?" the scrote called.

"Back here. Come."

Greg walked down the alley and got in the hire car. "Drive."

George pulled away, and Greg watched in the wing mirror. The kid got in the SUV and backed up.

"Can I sit up now?" Moon asked.

"No, stay down until we're at the hotel." Greg let out a long breath. "We need to pack and get the hell out of here."

"Bloody hell, no sightseeing?" George shook his head. "It'd look weirder if we go home now than if we stayed. Just give me one night in Amsterdam. I want to see what all the fuss is about."

Greg glanced at their bleach-speckled tracksuits. "Let's hope the receptionist thinks our gear's meant to look like this and it doesn't stand out as off. What I wouldn't do for an open fireplace now to burn it all."

George gave the glove box a rueful glance. "And a bag of lemon sherbets."

Chapter Sixteen

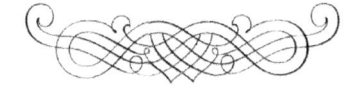

Ineke stood behind the door of Moeder's home office. A man had come, perhaps one of the naughty boyfriends. Ineke had been told to do her homework, to stay out of the way, but having seen the news this morning and how Moeder had drunk vodka all afternoon since she'd got back from the supermarket, she needed to know what was going on so she could prepare herself. Life so far with her mother had been

regimented, and she knew by the mood swings what would likely happen next. But this past week had thrown everything into confusion, and Ineke's tummy hurt from it clenching all the time. The unknown scared her.

She peered through the gap near the hinges.

"What the fuck are you doing, coming here?" Monster said. "And what's with the beard?"

The man, in an ill-fitting, too-tight suit, sat at the desk, his back to the door. "The police are being nosy. You gave me that phone to use, but I couldn't use it. I had to ditch the SIM."

"Why?"

"They came to mine, asking too many questions." He chuffed out a laugh. "That's why I squeezed into this suit to come and speak to you, why I've slapped a beard on. People around here would notice if I showed up in my jeans."

"At least you thought of that." Monster, sitting on the other side of the desk, smiled. "The last time I saw you in it you were in the dock."

"What, is that a reminder? You telling me why I only went to prison for two years?"

"No, I was reminiscing, nothing more." Monster disappeared as quickly as she always arrived, replaced

by Verdrietig. Tears fell. "I can't have it getting out that this was arranged by me."

He laughed. "It's not like I can afford to get caught either, Jesus."

"What did the police say?"

"They asked my whereabouts. My mother said I was at home, which is what she thought. She didn't know I climbed out of the window."

"So what's the problem?"

"The fact that they came to speak to me in the first place. I shouldn't even have been on their list. I haven't had anything to do with Sem for years. Not since…"

"Not since I put you both away."

"No. But they must have looked into him, seen we did that robbery together."

"So of course *you'd be on their list. Whether you cut yourself off from him or not, you have a past together."*

"Yeah, but it still pissed me off. Anyway, they wanted to know when I'd last seen him. I said it was down the bakery where he deals. I walked past, spotted him. I told them Dorothea and Sem were peddlers, which they were."

"Hmm, yet you didn't bother telling me."

"Look, what you asked me to do threw me, all right? I've been busy trying to get my shit together, then you turned up."

"Get your shit together? By doing what? Going straight?"

"Yeah, but it isn't working, so I'm having to rethink that."

"Or you got a thirst for crime again once you did that job for me."

"Maybe."

She took a tissue from a nearby box and dabbed her face. *"Where's the knife?"*

"In the canal."

"So they're going to find it. Please tell me you wore gloves."

"Of course I did! Christ!" He stuck a hand through his hair.

"Where's Sem?"

"In another part of the canal. I was stupid with Dorothea, I put her too close inland. I didn't think about it until she'd already gone under. So I dropped Sem nearer to the Amstel, so he might have moved into the river by now. They may never find him. He could stay under there forever."

"Shame you didn't think about that with Dorothea. Then it would have looked like they'd gone missing and

stayed that way. Since the police have a witness sighting of them together on Saturday night, they've joined the dots. They'll keep searching for Sem for God knows how long."

"They dealt drugs. It'll be put down to a dispute between dealers."

"You'd better be right."

"Is that a threat? You'd do well not to say shit like that to me, considering what I've done for you. If this gets pinned on me, I could go down for years."

"I'm not going to be telling anyone."

He leaned back. "When are you paying me the first instalment?"

"I sold one of my rings. Here." She opened the desk drawer and produced an envelope. "Once this has all died down, I'll be able to withdraw cash, but for now, it's best I don't do that. I had to rethink everything, and that was the only solution."

"Who did you sell it to? Could it come back to bite you?"

"I went to a certain pawnbroker who owes me."

"Ah. Right." He sniffed.

"Things are going to have to change now. My life. If it's true what Dorothea said, then people are watching me, and my ex said the same. I can't go out on Fridays."

"Do you want me to come here on those nights for a while? Save you going out and picking up your regulars?"

"Midnight."

"Fine."

"If anyone asks you where I am, say I've given up partying. People are apparently talking. I can't have my private business being known."

"Then you shouldn't have prowled the clubs."

With a swig of vodka from Moeder's favourite glass, Verdrietig vanished. "Don't tell me what I should and shouldn't have done." Monster glared at him. "I was in a bad place."

"For years?"

"Yes, for years. You'd never understand because you haven't been in love. My husband was everything to me."

"You need to get over him."

"Take the money and go. I can't…I can't deal with any more today."

Ineke ran to the kitchen and took a reading book out of her schoolbag. She sat at the island, glancing across at the man as he was leaving. He had his back to her again, so she couldn't see who he was. He stepped out into the street, Monster closing the door behind him.

Ineke pretended to read the book.

Monster rushed into the kitchen, grabbing the vodka bottle and gulping from it. She bent to take a plastic bag from a cupboard and tipped the contents onto the island. The pill packets. She ripped one open and removed the strips of tablets, pressing them out onto the surface. She repeated this with five packets, ten strips in all, and pushed the pills into a little mountain. She eyed the vodka bottle, then the tablets, biting her bottom lip hard enough that her teeth created white indents.

"Moeder says to watch her swallow all of these pills. Moeder says she will fall asleep and then stop breathing. Moeder says you must not phone Vader until *she stops breathing. Do you understand, Ineke?"*

"Why?"

"Because Moeder can't get her life together, that's why. It's pointless trying to continue if I can't go out anymore and pick up the boyfriends. No one loves me, so I may as well not be here." Tears fell. Verdrietig was back. "You will be sent to the cupboard, but it's what you deserve, so..." She laughed sadly. "You'll probably like it there better than here anyway."

She took a few of the tablets and put them in her mouth. Drank some vodka. She heaved. Maybe there were too many tablets to swallow, but she managed it in the end. Ineke stared, worrying about the cupboard and the nasty men and women who'd be in charge of her. She'd have to learn their ways so she didn't panic. If she knew what they were like, she could cope. Then, as Verdrietig put more pills on her tongue, Ineke snapped out of her selfish fear, another one taking its place. Moeder dying. Wasn't it better to be with her, here, even though she was horrible, than with strangers?

"Don't," she said. "Stop eating them, Mama!"

Verdrietig paused, the bottle of vodka to her lips. She smiled. Laughed. "It's too late. I've taken too many."

Ineke didn't like herself for sitting on the kitchen floor beside Moeder, waiting for her to stop breathing—she'd been told to do something, and she should do it. She wanted Moeder dead yet she didn't, and not knowing whether to disobey the order was giving her a headache. Her tears wouldn't stop, and she stroked Moeder's hair, pretending she was Lief, the woman who'd at least been kind to her. She wanted to go to sleep then wake up and find Monster raving—that was better than this, the house so still, the inside of her cheek bitten so much with worry that it bled.

A little while after Moeder had taken the tablets she'd been sick on the floor. She'd got up, weaving around, and pressed more tablets out of another packet. She'd taken them, then lay on the cold tiles, eyes closed.

The terror of being sent away, of Vader saying he didn't want her, pushed Ineke to her feet. She found Moeder's phone, the proper one, not the one she'd used to contact that man, and prodded Vader's number.

"What do you want, Evi?" he snapped.

"It's me."

"Ineke? What's happened?"

"Moeder took tablets and won't wake up."

"For fuck's— Right, listen to me. Put your fingers down her throat and make her sick."

"But she's already been sick."

"Good, that's something."

"But she took more tablets after."

"That fucking woman! Okay, right, do as I said and make her sick."

Ineke knelt beside Moeder. "Are you coming to help?"

"No, you can do this by yourself, you're a big girl."

Ineke put the phone on the floor. He wasn't coming. He didn't care.

Tears burned.

She had no choice. So she opened Moeder's mouth and stuck her small hand inside.

―――

No one came all weekend. Vader had phoned at eight on Monday morning to see how Moeder was—in bed, sleepy but alive. She didn't look well, and he'd said that would be because of the drugs. Ineke had wanted to phone the doctor or an ambulance, but Vader had said no. The less fuss on this, the better.

"I've phoned school and told them you're ill, and I've let our office know she won't be in. Take care of her this week—soup, you can manage to get that out of a can, can't you?"

"What about the cleaning lady and the woman who makes our food?"

"Christ…Evi doesn't even cook or do housework?" A sigh. "You can open the door to them, let them in, but tell the cleaner not to go into your mother's room, and tell them you're both unwell."

"Moeder won't speak to me. She's asleep a lot."

"That will be her body's way of fixing her. Did you clean up the sick?"

"Yes."

"And you threw the pills and drink away like I told you? All of it?"

"Yes."

"Right, well, I'll leave you to it, then."

By Friday night, Moeder was much better, although she stayed in bed as Verdrietig, crying, saying she couldn't even get that right, killing herself. Vader had said it would be a wonder if she hadn't ruined her liver and kidneys with what she'd done, but as long as she lived until Ineke was old enough to stay by herself, what did he care?

Ineke lay in bed, staring at the dark ceiling, wishing she had a different mother and father, a life where she hadn't had to nurse a woman who didn't want to be here anymore. A woman who'd been willing to let her go into the starvation cupboard. A father who hadn't taken this burden away from her, instead letting her carry it on her own.

The doorbell rang, and she shot up to check the clock beside the bed. Midnight.

Oh God, had that man come? The one in the too-small suit?

She got out of bed, making it to the landing, and there was Moeder, poised at the top of the stairs, one hand on the post. This was the first time she'd left her bedroom other than to use the bathroom.

"Go back to bed. Shut your door."
Ineke obeyed.
A boyfriend. Maybe he could save Moeder. Maybe everything would be all right now.

Chapter Seventeen

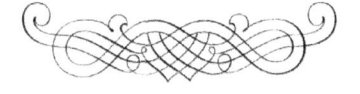

Ineke had let the London men into her room. George had explained everything that had happened at the house, and the relief at not having to worry about Christoffel being hurt or killed was so immense she'd sunk to the chair at the desk and sobbed into her hands. Wrung out now, she inspected her feelings about men being dead, plus an innocent drug dealer who'd got caught up in this. Would their phones be found where Greg had put them on the way here? Would any cameras have picked up the fact he'd got out of the hire car, used a bin, then driven off? Would that come back to bite everyone on the backside?

But the deaths. Was it okay to feel bad but at the same time not care they were dead? They were gone, nothing could change that, and whoever they'd left behind, loved ones, would soon be rolling around in grief, but was that her problem? Didn't she have enough traumas of her own to deal with? Adding more to the mix, she might find herself tipped over the edge into insanity.

The house had been scrubbed and bleached, so hopefully nothing of her would be left behind from when she'd chatted to Hendrik about the UK proposition, but then she'd never been arrested, so no fingerprints taken, no DNA swab. She'd been in this hotel, out of the way for days, so she wouldn't be a suspect, and she'd be on CCTV when she left here, showing she hadn't exited the building to kill anyone, but it still didn't stop her from worrying about it.

"How do you feel?" Greg asked.

"Happy but guilty."

"Hmm, I can understand that." He peered out of the window. Maybe he was just as paranoid as her about something going wrong and he wanted to double-check a stray member of Hendrik's team wasn't out there spying, a man they didn't know about, like the one with the moped. "We'll go home tomorrow, but how do you fancy having one last night out in Amsterdam? You can show us the best places to go."

Ineke hadn't been out to have fun, not since the night after she'd left home and had got so drunk she'd thrown up in the street. The pull to be with these men—especially Greg—was a big draw, but...what if Moeder was out, too? What if they bumped into her?

"My mother. She...likes to drink and pick men up. She might have stopped all that, but...she could be in the city."

"We'll go and see her now, if you like," George said. "Warn her she isn't welcome to go out tonight. I'll *make* the bitch stay in."

Moon held a finger up. "For the record, I've had enough weed and partying to last me a lifetime, and given the fact I haven't been in disguise, it's best I sit this one out, keep my head down by staying in the hotel until we go to the airport."

George nodded. "Glad you said that. I don't fancy an old man trotting round with us."

"Why don't you shut your mush?" Moon said. "I'll have you know I've still got it in me, I just don't want to go. And while I'm holding the microphone, change the colour of your beards and glasses before you gallivant all around the pubs—I take it you've brought a selection with you. Leave here clean-shaven and slap them on in an alley, then get them off before you come back in." He tutted. "Don't look at me like I'm teaching you to suck eggs, George. If those bodies get found earlier than we'd like, the coppers are going to be looking for two blokes with black beards. And for the record, I think you're taking a risk by going out, so don't say I didn't warn you if it all goes tits up."

George stood from the bed and moved towards his brother. "Shall we take him down and batter him with a pillow?"

Greg laughed. "Nah, knowing our luck he'll have a heart attack."

"Fuck off, the pair of you," Moon growled.

Ineke soaked in the dynamics between these men. It was clear they were joking, Moon pretending to be angry, but she found it difficult to process. People who said what could be considered cruel things but didn't really mean them, she'd never experienced it until now. Monster had meant them, and jokes were far from the relationship Ineke had had with her, and as for Vader, he barely cracked a smile and seemed more intent on his daughter being a good example to him than anything else.

It saddened her, how much she'd missed out on. Laughter. A sense of camaraderie.

"You all right, love?" Greg asked.

Shocked at him being so perceptive in picking up her mood, giving enough of a shit to check in with her, she said, "Just...thinking."

"About your old dear?"

"Yes."

"We don't have to pay her a visit if you don't want to."

Ineke sighed. "Maybe I *should* go and see her for the last time. There's never been a resolution, I just moved out without telling her."

"If you think it will do any good," George said. "But people like her don't admit when they've done wrong because they think what they're doing is right. Fair warning, if she's nasty to you, I'll punch her lights out."

"George!" Moon stood. "Watch yourself. You're not in London now. There can't be a mark on that woman that she can show the coppers. I'll be in my room. Ring me when you're back tonight so I can sleep okay."

"All right, Dad," George said.

"Knob off, seriously." Moon left, closing the door quietly behind him.

"Are you three always like this?" Ineke asked.

"Ah, he loves it," George said. "So, where does your mother live?"

Ineke told them. "We should get a tram; it won't stop us from being seen on it, and there is CCTV on the streets, but when we get to her house, we will be safe unless people have got security cameras up. The hire car might have a route recorder."

George stared at Greg. "Fuck, I didn't think of that. We've been to that house…"

Greg sighed. "Bollocks. We can't take it to a garage and pay someone to fuck it up because there's no one we can trust here. We're just going to have to wing it and hope me doctoring the number plate throws the police off—if they even become involved."

"Right, let's go." George moved towards the door.

"Can we wait until it is dark when we go there?" Ineke asked. "She will not be home from work yet anyway."

"Fair enough. We'll leave you be, then. We'll be back about six, all right?" Greg smiled. "Do you want to change and whatever before we go?"

"I do not have any clothes other than these and pyjamas. Hendrik said he would buy me new in England. My studio flat...he said he would move all my things out and sell it for me. Give me the money. But he did not."

"Fuck me, he really *did* want you to work for him, didn't he?" George kicked the wall. "Conniving bastard."

Ineke stood, the clothes she had on the same ones as when Hendrik had brought her here. They needed washing. Maybe, if Moeder was Lief and in a good mood, she'd allow her to take some things she'd left behind when she'd moved out. She could perhaps get dressed up in her old bedroom while Lief pretended to the twins she was a nice person.

But was it safe to leave her with George? Surely he wouldn't do anything silly. Moeder was a judge, she'd be missed by Monday morning if she didn't turn up for work.

Ineke prayed all would go well. That the only thing to happen would be that she came away feeling wretched like she had as a child.

She could cope with that.

It was safe.

Chapter Eighteen

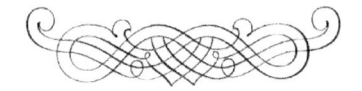

In a striking red dress and matching high heels, reminding Ineke of the past, Moeder stood on the threshold. She hadn't been able to hide her shock and confusion at seeing Ineke on her doorstep, her mouth working with no words coming out. She'd quickly cottoned on that Ineke wasn't alone but with two hulking, identical men, one each side of her. Both had rubber gloves on, hidden behind their backs. Ineke didn't want to ask herself why they'd worn them. Didn't want to imagine murder might happen here. Didn't want to have to admit, yet, that she was coming round to the idea. Whether she'd want to be present while they did it remained to be seen.

"We are using English today, Moeder. These men do not speak Dutch."

The charming Lief smile appeared. "Darling! It has been so *long*. Where have you *been*? You left without a word, and I have been so *worried*."

Ineke didn't respond. She didn't trust herself to. The stress on the words at the end of sentences grated on her nerves. So many accusations — *truths* — bubbled up on her tongue, sticking in her throat, swirling in her head, waiting for her to release them. Spiteful things, designed to hurt, but what would be the point? She'd have gone down to Moeder's level by doing that, and anyway, whatever she said wouldn't affect the woman. She had no feelings except those she nurtured for herself — self-pity, fake sorrow as Verdrietig, who wasn't *really* apologetic to Ineke about what she'd done, the platitudes hollow, devoid of any true emotion, nothing like the type a mother *should* feel towards her daughter. No, the only reason Verdrietig was sad was because she lamented the fact she'd had a child in the first place.

"Come in," Lief said, all smiles.

Stepping into her childhood home sent an immediate shiver down Ineke's back. It was exactly the same as it had always been—Moeder hadn't changed a thing since Vader had left, a sure sign she couldn't let go, that she wanted everything suspended in time in the hope her husband would return, slotting back in as if he'd never left, like a misplaced photo to be hung on the empty space on the wall that it had previously occupied. It was creepy, it proved Moeder had mental health issues that needed to be addressed. Should Ineke feel sorry for her because of that? Did a woman who needed help deserve to be exonerated for everything she'd done?

No, Moeder had stopped taking the tablets by choice and turned to drink and treating Ineke like shit as her props instead. Her selfish attitude towards Ineke, blaming her for being alive, the core of all her troubles, was still a nasty thing to do whether her mind was messed up or not. She'd made conscious decisions in how she'd treated her daughter, and no amount of diagnoses could alter that. You could be fucked up in the head and still be sane at the same time.

She'd known what she was doing, on some level.

Lief led them to the kitchen, her heels clip-clopping, the signal from Ineke's childhood that Dorothea would be arriving soon for her hair-do, her nails being done, her private area trimmed. As an adult, Ineke still couldn't comprehend the old woman expecting that of her.

Lief took vodka out of the cupboard along with four glasses. "Drink?"

"Not for us," George said.

He gave her such an evil stare that Ineke wouldn't want to get on his bad side. Lief frowned at him. And how lovely it was for Ineke to not want to step in and make things better, to smooth any ruffles—to know she didn't *need* to anymore. Moeder wasn't her problem, hadn't been for two years, and only now she was back did Ineke realise how less stressed she'd been while living by herself, yet at the time she'd thought she *was* stressed. The old feelings hovered behind her, though, ghosts of the past waiting to sit on her shoulders and push them down, to settle in their familiar spot as though they'd missed tormenting her. But she wouldn't allow them the privilege to climb aboard. Doing that returned the control to Moeder, and she would *not* let that happen.

"Oh," Lief said, breezy. "Okay, just me then." She poured enough vodka that showed she definitely planned to go out on the town tonight. Why would she do that when she'd switched it to the boyfriends visiting her instead? Perhaps there was a work party.

Ineke automatically made a move to sit at the island but stopped herself at the last minute, remembering George's warning on the tram: "Touch nothing in that house, just in case. If you want to collect clothes, ask us to pick them up for you. We've got gloves, you haven't."

"So!" Lief smiled brightly. "How have you *been*, Ineke?"

I wonder if she wanted to call me Little Slave. "Busy."

"I can imagine. All those studies and standing behind glass at night."

So she's kept tabs on me. Ineke shuddered. "My life is mine to do what I want with, what I choose. I don't have to follow what you and Vader expect."

"I would never suggest such a thing. You are your own person, darling."

"I see you're still good at pretending, like you did with Vader," Ineke said. "Why bother when these men know what you did to me?"

"What I did?" Lief laid a hand on her chest.

Ineke sighed. "You're going to fake your way through this conversation? I should have known."

Lief appealed to George and Greg. "I am sorry about my daughter, she has an overactive imagination, always has loved to spin stories. She should have been a writer not a whore."

The mask had slipped. Lief flinched.

George took a step towards her, but Greg stood in the way to keep him back. Lief frowned again, as though she didn't understand why George had done that.

What was going on?

Lief took a gulp of alcohol. She stared at Ineke, Monster lurking. Then she looked at George. "Why did Hendrik lie to me?"

Ineke's skin turned cold, goosebumps springing up, the hairs on her head seeming to quiver in their follicles. The confusion on the doorstep made sense now, horrible, disgusting sense. Moeder had been shocked to see her daughter because she *wasn't supposed to be there.* She was meant to be dead, Moon her killer. She *knew.* She fucking *knew* all along. What kind of mother arranged that? What kind of mother hated her child that much she was prepared to let her die?

Ineke swallowed. Glanced at George. He'd realised what was going on, too, as had Greg who clenched his hands into fists behind his back, his rubber gloves squeaking. Moeder had no clue she'd just walked herself into a nightmare.

"That was you?" Ineke asked, successfully keeping a tremor from her voice. She couldn't let this woman know she'd shocked her. Although why she'd asked for confirmation she didn't know. She didn't need any. It was so obvious now why Hendrik had chosen her.

Lief flashed her perfect teeth. "Of course. I know shady people, you are aware of that. I am so surprised he lied to me, though. You were meant to be dead ages ago. He said you were."

George brought his hand out in front of him, flexing the gloves. Lief stared at them, clearly baffled, then tittered to disguise her discomfort.

"Oh, how *wonderful!*" She laughed, her head thrown back. "You're going to kill her *now*, if front of *me*? What a wonderful *gift!*" Her forehead scrunched. "I still don't understand him lying, though. What is the point in doing that?" This had been said as if to herself, Moeder sorting through her thoughts, trying to get them to make sense. "He said you were strangled."

"Obviously, I wasn't." Ineke didn't have the pleasure of sifting through her own thoughts because one stood out above the rest, drowning the others out with its loud shriek: *Let George kill her...* "Why would you tell him to do that?"

Lief bordered on morphing into Monster, the telltale signs of her expression giving the game away. A tic here, a flutter of an eyelid there. "Didn't I always say you should never have been born? I wanted you aborted like you should have been all those years ago." She smiled at the twins. "Get on with it, then, but no blood. I really do not want any evidence in my house."

"How did you know Hendrik?" Ineke asked. "Or maybe I already know. He was in your court for some crime or other, wasn't he, but I bet you let him go."

"Hmm. Let's just say I found where a certain person was and decided to play a little game. I asked that Bart killed you, but it is clear my instructions were not followed. Hendrik could go far—*if* he listens to me. *If* he does not lie to me. I could have him taken out inside a second for pretending you were dead. I really must ask him why he did that."

"Because he needed her for another deal he's got on the go," George said. "He played you."

Lief finished her vodka and poured more, cleverly hiding any annoyance. "Are you *sure* you do not want one, gentlemen?"

"I've already said no," George snapped.

Lief-almost-Monster glared at him. "I suggest you do not speak to me like that." She narrowed her eyes. "When did you join Hendrik's little gang? I was not aware he had brought Englishmen into the fold. That is where you are from, isn't it?"

Ineke smiled. *She* was in control now, the twins were, not her mother. And knowing Lief wasn't aware yet, it was liberating. When would the penny drop?

George casually rounded the island and took Moeder by the shoulders, turning her to face him.

He did it gently, hiding his true intent, and Lief gazed up at him.

"I bet you are good-looking under that beard," she whispered. "The kind of man who knows how to treat a lady in bed."

How desperate can she be to fling herself at him like that?

George leaned his head closer to hers and slid one hand to the base of her throat. "I bet you're an expensive shag." He moved his hand higher. "I bet you know how to please a man for the right price." Higher still. "Just like the whore you pretend not to be. The woman who goes out at night and brings conquests back, then tells her little girl about them the next day. Sick bitch."

Lief's eyes widened in understanding, that shiny penny falling, falling, falling, landing on the floor to spin and spin on its edge along with her racing thoughts. Too late. Too fucking late to get away from him because he jerked her around so the lip of the island almost dug into her back. Bent her over into an uncomfortable position, his other hand at the base of her spine, perhaps so the edge didn't mark her skin and leave proof of what he could have done. His touch on her throat was light; he didn't want to leave bruises.

"If I put pressure on your chest," he said, "your back will snap."

Her eyelashes fluttered. "Why are you doing this? Did Hendrik tell you to?"

"I wouldn't do a thing that man said. Anyway, he's dead. All of them are. We never worked for him, we work for ourselves. For Ineke."

Lief laughed. "Bart is dead, too? Oh, how amusing." She sobered. "Get your fucking filthy hands off me," Monster snarled, finally out for all to see. "You do not get to touch me like this, to threaten me, and get away with it."

"Who's going to stop me?" George drew her away from the island and turned her, holding her back to his front, his hand on her neck moving down to between her collarbones, the other on her stomach. "This is how things are going to go. You're going to say sorry to your daughter." He paused. Whispered, "Even if you don't mean it, make it sound like you do."

"Never! She does not deserve to be here after what she put me through."

"What, by just being alive, an innocent kid? You nasty piece of scum bitch. Ineke?"

He glanced at her, and she nodded. Oh God, she nodded.

"Greg, get me one of those knives," George ordered.

Moeder kicked back at his shins, spitting low curses, her hair swinging, her face perspiring. "I swear to God…"

"Swear all you like, the result will be the same."

Ineke had thought she'd want to stop this, to shout and say no, but she remained where she was, fascinated that her mother was so out of her depth, that the realisation she was going to die had now taken all the fight out of her. Fascinated by these men, how they worked together so seamlessly. Did Moeder *want* to end it all? The torment she must go through every day? Was it better for her to let someone else do it so she didn't have to make the decision, so she didn't have to muster up the courage?

How odd, to be her. To be so cruel yet pitiful at the same time. To be an ogre yet a woman who needed help for her mental state. To be Ineke, who wanted Monster dead, just like Monster and all of her personalities had wanted Ineke dead.

Does that make me a bad person? To want this to end?

Greg pulled a long knife from the block on the worktop by the microwave. George manoeuvred Moeder to the floor, ordering her to sit. She crumpled down, obeying someone for once, resigned to her fate. Welcoming it, even.

George took the knife and crouched behind her. "You know what to do, bruv."

Greg went down on his haunches, took Moeder's forearm and held it out over her lap, as if she planned to slit the wrist herself.

"Is she left- or right-handed?" George asked.

"Right," Ineke said, appalled yet thankful he'd thought of such a thing; a mistake there could have tipped the police off to something being wrong.

"Good." George made the slice then quickly placed his other hand over Monster's mouth, muffling her scream of pain.

Would that leave bruises? Would the police know someone else had been here? Or would they get lucky and this would be viewed as Moeder taking her own life? Would there be a post-mortem anyway because it had been a suicide? Would there? Had anyone seen them arrive? Would they remember the car? Did they have a video doorbell?

George placed the knife in Moeder's right hand as she stared down at her wrist. Blood flowed in a dark sheet onto her crimson dress. Her breathing stuttered, and she glanced across at Ineke, a smile on her spiteful, red-painted mouth.

"Will you lick the floor when I'm gone?"

Ineke steeled her heart so those words didn't hurt, surprised to find they didn't. Variations of them had been spat at her over the years, her worthlessness, the hassle of her being in Moeder's life, in Vader's, her presence the reason he'd walked out on them. Never Moeder's fault.

The evil woman smiled. "This should have been you, little slave."

"No," Ineke said. "It should always have been you."

Chapter Nineteen

The city streets, packed with people, had a vibe like no other. Even in London, the crowds didn't generate this kind of buzz, as if the air were alive, breathing, laughing along with those off their face on booze or weed, or people just high on the natural endorphins being away from home infused them with. The main District. A building called Moulin Rouge, and another that offered live sex shows. Red lights everywhere. Drinkers sitting at tables in front of coffee shops even in winter. The canal twinkling with scarlet reflections, the arch of a nearby bridge adorned with more red bulbs. All of it was an abrupt slap to the senses.

George, never one to go out on a bender and soak in the atmosphere, and despite their recent antics looming over them, for once decided to let half his guard down. Ineke, in a black dress and shoes she'd taken from that bitch's house, her dirty items in a large handbag, led the way through the too-thick crowd, people standing around in clusters, men on a stag do obvious. Somewhere along here, he'd bet women serviced customers behind the darkened glass of those upper windows in rented rooms.

On the way here, down an alley, he'd been brought up short by the sight of a lady to his left, behind a full-length pane, sitting on a high stool in her underwear and filing her nails. He'd known this went on here, but it still shocked him to see the outright offer of sex, how explicit it was. Farther on, another woman had scrolled her phone, as though people didn't gawp in at her and give her a mental rating to see if she was worthy enough of their euros, to let them paw her. His immediate reaction was to help them, to get them out of this life, or at least pay for them to go to London and let Debbie look after them if the oldest profession was the one they wanted, but Ineke had explained this was just a normal job here. For the most part they were safe and doing this of their own free will.

He still couldn't get his head around it, the legality of it. It felt wrong to be amongst this, to be allowed to approach a window and barter the terms without looking over your shoulder to check if the plod lurked nearby. All the police here seemed to be interested in was ensuring no one smoked weed on the streets (signs reinforced the rule) and making sure no one started trouble. Then there were the Angels in their matching polo shirts and jackets, people assigned to watch out for anyone who needed help—to get back to their hotel, to use a phone, to report a crime, to ask for an ambulance or a bottle of water to sober up.

It gave him the idea to create an Angel team on Cardigan, polo-shirted wingmen who swooped in to lend the residents a hand.

Ineke weaved to the left, waiting by a gathering of drinkers at a pub door. He wasn't going to partake in any weed, fuck that, but a beer wouldn't hurt. She walked inside, and he followed, catching sight of his blond beard and matching wig as a reflection in the purple-lit window, Greg at his back. Inside, the tables full, music playing, the air thick with cannabis smoke and chatter. This city must make a fortune.

They drank Heineken and chatted, Ineke revealing more snippets from her past that boiled George's blood. A couple of beers later, he relaxed enough to shoot the shit with some Londoners here on holiday, as if he wasn't one of The Brothers. Greg mellowed enough to dance with Ineke. George hadn't picked up on any attraction between them until now, but there was something there. He shrugged it off—it could just be the booze giving Greg permission to let loose, he might not fancy her at all. But if he did, George wouldn't complain. Ineke deserved happiness, to be looked after, and what better person to do it than his brother?

Maybe his near-death experience has given him a different perspective.

The night wore on, and seven bottles of Heineken in, George needed to stop. He wasn't drunk, just pleasantly tipsy, but what wits he still had about him he wanted to keep.

Back out amongst the throng, the atmosphere even more charged with weed-infused happiness than before, he linked his arm with Ineke, Greg on her other side, because she was off her face and in need of help to walk. Neither George nor Greg had stopped her from downing shots—they'd killed her mother, for fuck's sake, and even though Ineke had given the nod, seeing it, smelling that blood, combined with the no-doubt conflicting feelings going through her, she'd still have needed to blot it out.

They took a cab to the hotel, asking the driver to drop them in the underground car park (so they could take their beards and wigs off before entering reception). Thankfully, Ineke appeared a little more with it by the time they made it to the lobby, and George needn't have worried. The night-time receptionist didn't even bother to look up from her phone.

They deposited Ineke in her room, on the bed. The only thing Greg took off were her shoes.

George hung her handbag on the back of the desk chair, Greg sitting in the one by the window.

"I'll sleep here," he said. "In case she's sick in the night."

George nodded. "That all right with you, Ineke?"

"Yeah," came the slurred reply. "I like Greg. He's pretty."

"Pretty?" George laughed. "Pretty ugly."

"Err, you do realise we look the same," Greg said. "So that means you're ugly, too."

"Bog off." George nodded to his pointing-shit-out twin. "Reckon I should fill Moon in on what happened at her mother's?"

"Probably best he's brought up to speed. He did say to give him a ring when we got in. A knock's just the same."

George left, taking the stairs to Moon's floor. He tapped on the door.

Moon answered in just his boxer shorts, ushering him inside and closing the door. "What have you done?"

George grinned. "Never mind me, what has *Debbie* done by shacking up with you? Look at the state of you in them kecks…"

Moon glowered. "Debbie happens to like my body just the way it is, belly an' all, so fuck right off. Answer me."

"How do you even know we've done anything?"

"Your face. I *know* you, son." Moon sighed. "Do I need to pour a brandy for this? Open the window so I can have a cigar?"

"Maybe." George sat on the bed. "Depends on whether you're likely to hit the roof or not and need something to take the edge off."

Moon plonked onto a chair. "Come on, out with it."

"I killed Ineke's mother."

"Oh, fuck me sideways. You just couldn't behave, could you."

"You'd have done the same in my shoes if you saw what she's like. She's the one who sent Hendrik Ineke's way. What an utter fucking cow."

"What? Jesus…that poor girl, having a mother like that."

"I did it so it looks like the bitch killed herself. She was weird at the end, though, stopped struggling, like she agreed that I should slit her wrist."

"You risked *blood*? Lord almighty. What the hell's *wrong* with you?"

George shrugged. "Calm your man tits—and you *do* have man tits, just so you know."

"I'm warning you, George... Don't test me."

"All right, all right. I couldn't be arsed to find any rope or whatever to string her up with, okay? I don't think I got any on me anyway, and these clothes are black, so..."

Moon walked to the window, as if the whole of Amsterdam stood out there, questioning them and what they'd done here, and he needed to see it, to feel the weight of their verdict. "There'll be uproar. She's a prominent judge."

"Yep, I'm aware of that. Greg didn't stop me, so don't just blame me for this. While she was getting rat-arsed, Ineke told us about this old woman who used to babysit her. Dorothea. If she wasn't already dead, I'd be going after her an' all, I can tell you. But Dorothea used to say stuff to her, about what the mother got up to, and one of the things that stuck in Ineke's head was that people were beginning to talk, that the mum was sleeping with men she shouldn't be, and it wouldn't be long before she was caught. Ineke remembered hearing a conversation about it between her mum and dad, too."

"So you reckon her father will mention it, he'll suggest to the police that one of the men she used to see had forced her to slash her wrist?"

"Or a group of them. A group of three."

"To cover up the fact the three of you might have been seen going inside her gaff?"

"Yeah."

"But that means getting word to her dad."

George nodded. "Too risky?"

"Yeah. Debbie's booked our flights for nine in the morning. Let's just go home and forget all about this, eh?"

George sighed. Sometimes, Moon knew his onions. "I think Greg's got a thing for Ineke."

"I did wonder when I saw the way he was looking at her earlier. She likes him, too. Could just be a saviour complex or whatever the fuck it's called when someone helps them out of a tight spot."

"It's more than a tight spot, it's a fucking nightmare. Her whole life has been."

"Vic will help her through."

George couldn't argue with that. "Yeah, it'll all come out in the wash as our mum used to say."

But this trip would linger in his mind for a long time. He'd be waiting for a copper to knock on his door at any point, the link made between them being in Amsterdam and what had happened. But it would be all right, they'd have the new pig, Bryan Flint, on their side to warn them of any danger coming their way so they could get their stories straight. Failing that, Janine would still keep an eye out for them until she went on maternity leave.

We've still got to approach Flint yet. Get him round to our way of thinking.

He sighed. Said goodnight too Moon.

Time for bed.

Chapter Twenty

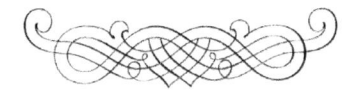

*V*ader had come to collect Ineke. She was so tired from looking after Moeder and wished she didn't have to go. But Moeder was sort of back to being her nasty self so wouldn't let her catch up on sleep anyway. The other worry was that if Ineke left, would Moeder take tablets again? Would Vader ring the bell on their return and get no answer? Would he have to break the door down to get inside? It was so strange, *to want to keep her mother alive yet hate her at the same time. Or was she being selfish in not wanting to go into the starvation cupboard? With no one to talk to about this, she couldn't see what was right and wrong or how she was supposed to feel.*

Confused by her emotions, the way they swung to and fro, she crept from the kitchen, where she'd been told to stay, and quietly took her coat and shoes from the cupboard in the foyer while Lief spoke to Vader at the door. Always Lief when he called by. Always pretending everything was all right.

"How have you been?" Vader asked.

"I tried to kill myself," Lief whispered.

"I know."

"How?"

"Ineke phoned me. She was the one who saved you."

Ineke could have cried. Vader shouldn't have said that. Moeder had been complaining the past day or so that if her body hadn't rejected the tablets, she'd have got what she wanted—oblivion, as she'd put it, and then Vader would be sorry and realise what he'd lost too late, but it would punish him, and that was her aim. But now she knew it was Ineke's fault, something else to blame her for.

"She never said. Oh, how awful for her to have found me, poor girl. What did she do?"

"She rang me. Told me what you'd done, that she'd seen it, Evi. I told her to make you sick, and I rather think it's awful for you to have tried to take your own life when your child is present in the first place. You disgust me."

"My life is so hard…"

"Is it? Is it really? Or are you making it hard? If you took your tablets, it would be a damn sight easier."

"I did take the tablets." There was a smile in her voice.

"Not like that," Vader snapped. *"I should get her taken away from you."*

"Why don't you?" Lief twirled her hair. *"Oh, that's right, you don't want our little secret to come out."*

Ineke froze in slipping on a shoe. What secret?

"We've discussed this," Vader said, *"and going over it time and again won't change anything. What we're doing is the best thing for everyone, we agreed on that."*

"I only agreed because I didn't have any other choice. By the time you found out, she was two. I have to admit, you're a gentleman for what you're doing, and I am *grateful."*

"Are you? What would have happened if you hadn't woken up? If you'd died?"

"You would have taken her."

"You know it wouldn't be legal for me to do that."

"But no one would have known..."

"I would have. It's all well and good me doing fatherly things with her, but we both know I'm not who she thinks I am. He would have had to take her."

He?

"No. Never." Lief switched to Verdrietig, *"Please, I'm begging you..."*

"Like you begged me not to tell him about her?" Vader leaned closer and whispered, *"You slept with the bloody electrician while I was on that course. You couldn't get more cliché if you tried. Woman lets workman in and seduces him. Christ, Evi. You spend all your time blaming Ineke for being born, me for leaving you when I finally found out, when you should be looking at yourself. You opened your legs to him, no one else. You were the one to break our marriage vows. It's your fault, all yours, and I refuse to take the blame anymore."*

Verdrietig moved even closer. *"Just kiss me so you remember how it was between us. Then you'll come home."*

"You're deranged, Evi, you're not well, and you need to get help. That child deserves better."

"Then you should have stayed so she wasn't left alone with me."

"I couldn't, not after I knew. I only play this part so she isn't hurt, but I shouldn't have to. She has *a father, someone who might well give her what she needs, because I'm sorry, I can't."*

"What are you saying? That you're going to walk away for good? What will people think?"

"That was my problem back then. I cared what they thought. Them knowing what you did, how you couldn't even put your sex addiction to one side for the couple of nights I was away. And to be so stupid as to get yourself pregnant when we used condoms and I'd query it. How dumb I was, believing one had split. Do you know why? Because I wanted to believe we had the perfect thing going, and we didn't. I went along with everything so I didn't get pitying looks, but I wish I hadn't."

"It's Ineke's fault for getting ill."

Vader shook his head. "Have you listened to yourself? You're blaming a two-year-old child for being ill? So it's her fault the blood tests showed…you know what they showed. You are not *right in the head. As for Greet, she knows everything, so don't think you can cook up some scheme to split us up."*

"You told her?"

"Yes, right from day one, and she agreed to play along with us for the sake of your *child. Don't do this*

again, don't overdose or slit your wrists or whatever the hell you have in mind, do you understand? Sort your fucking life out. If I hear about you messing around with pills, I'll find him—and I'll tell him."

"No, please..."

"Why, because you want this charade to continue? So you get to see me on your doorstep once a month, picking up a child that belongs to another...I can't even think what to call him so Ineke doesn't question it if she's listening. A rook. And besides, you see me enough at work."

"But we don't talk there. We do here."

Vader shook his head. "Honestly, you are unwell. Find help." He stepped back. "Ineke, time to go."

She struggled to understand what she'd heard, to make sense of it. Who was the electrician? And why would Moeder go to sleep with him? Had she been tired? What was a rook? And a charade?

She walked to the door. Lief had gone, and Verdrietig cried softly. She'd go and be Monster after they'd left, Ineke was sure of it.

"Ice cream at the cinema after bowling?" Vader asked. "I think you need a treat after everything your mother's put you through." He glared at Verdrietig. "Crocodile tears. They don't work with me, not anymore."

He led Ineke towards his car, a hand on her shoulder.

"What's a rook?" she asked.

He glanced away. "No one, unfortunately for me. Come on."

Ineke jumped out of her thoughts as the flight attendant announced for the seat belts to be put on. She blinked, her memories still uppermost in her mind, and clipped herself in. She'd forgotten all about that day, but it seemed her mind wanted her to remember now. Maybe it knew she was strong enough to face it, to read between the lines and understand what had happened. All those words—how had her mind stored them? How had it been so clever as to hide them from her?

"He's not my father," she blurted to Greg beside her.

"Who?"

"The man I thought was my father…wasn't."

He winced. "Been there, done that. How do you know?"

She told him. "So that means Christoffel isn't my brother."

That hurt more, that the one thing she'd thought belonged to her…didn't.

Greg placed a hand on hers. "Listen, if you ever want to talk, say so. This is a lot to unpack."

"All this time, she blamed me, when it was her."

"It was always her. No mother should treat their child like that or blame them for being born. And your dad, well, the bloke you thought was your dad, I bet it makes sense now why he was so distant emotionally."

"I wonder what he'd say if I told him I know." She laughed at her younger self. "I even asked him what a rook was, so he must have known I'd heard everything, yet he never brought it up again."

"The pair of them are fucked up, to be honest. I mean, yeah, he took you out as if he was your dad, but other than that, he wasn't exactly model father material, was he. You said he was bothered about what people thought if they found out your mum had cheated. What a wanker." Greg rested his head back. "We have so much in common you wouldn't believe."

"How?"

"I'll tell you about it one day. A story about a man called Richard."

Her mind whirred. Who was her father? Did she even want to find out? From what she'd gathered from the memory, he didn't even know she existed. He'd probably have his own family now and wouldn't want her muscling in.

She closed her eyes on the descent. Focused on what was going to happen next so she didn't have to think about the past, how glad she was that Moeder was dead, how angry she was that Vader had lied about who he was. She'd be staying with Moon and Debbie until her flat was sorted, and she forced herself to concentrate on settling in London, leaving Amsterdam behind.

That place was full of nightmares, and all she wanted now were pleasant dreams.

She squeezed Greg's hand.

He squeezed back.

Chapter Twenty-One

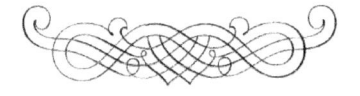

On Monday, Ineke stood in the kitchen of a two-bed, ground-floor flat in the East End. The row of houses had been converted, and this one used to be student digs, apparently, until they'd bought it. It seemed fitting, her being a student soon, to live here. Fate, perhaps. It came fully furnished with a garden, but only she could use that. A table-and-chair set sat on the flagstones visible through the patio doors, so different from Amsterdam—no decking, no revelling neighbours opposite, no people sailing past on barges with their bottles of beer. England was so…full of land, as far as she'd seen. Maybe she'd get to see the Thames soon.

According to George that was standard, the furniture coming with it, but he'd lied. Funny how certain lies were okay, they were good. She'd overheard Moon on the phone yesterday, saying it was "Bloody nice of you to buy everything for her…was it Greg's idea by any chance?" The place smelled of newness—paint, the sofas, everything. They must have kitted it out while she'd been staying with Moon and Debbie.

She hadn't seen the twins since Saturday when they'd landed, although Greg had put his personal number in her phone, which he'd found at the base house, as well as their business one, and messaged her to make sure she was okay over the weekend. She'd smiled every time—to have someone caring about her was strange, a little overwhelming if she were honest, what with George doing the same, plus Moon and Debbie fussing over her. Nothing was too much trouble. A horrible part of her, the Moeder side that must live inside her somewhere, passed on through the genes, worried that this was all a bribe, to get her to keep her mouth shut about what they'd done in Amsterdam.

They needn't have bothered. She wasn't about to tell anyone. And besides, they acted like a family towards her—or what she'd imagined was a family. Unable to go to schoolfriends' houses, she hadn't seen what it was like in other homes, and as for Vader, she couldn't base what a family was like on that trio because she'd only seen them together that time she'd visited their black house.

Waking up to find Greg sleeping in the hotel chair in Amsterdam had confused her to begin with, then she'd remembered how drunk she'd been and that he'd stayed there in case she was sick. That had been a first. Moeder hadn't done that, ever, even when Ineke was ill, and it just went to show that it was true: some people could care about your welfare more than your own parents.

She'd expected today to be awkward for some reason—Greg on home soil, his attraction to her in Amsterdam only because he was away, a holiday thing, but no, it seemed it was still there, going by the way he looked at her now.

"Do you like it?" he asked, pensive. "We can get you a bigger place if you need it."

"No, no." She shook her head. "This is perfect, thank you. How much is the rent?"

She could afford to live here. Debbie had offered her the job of taking over the night-time shift on Kitchen Street to replace a lady called Sharny who'd died at the hands of a serial killer. No sex involved if she didn't want it—Ineke's role was to oversee the women, report anything out of the ordinary, and ensure each of them came back after being with clients. Debbie had shown her their system, the log of all 'punters' and the WhatsApp group where the women chatted to let the others know where they were while working and when they were back on Kitchen.

Ineke had accepted. Debbie had also signed her up and paid for an Open University course so Ineke could finish her studies. It was lovely to have people who gave a shit about her, to want to do everything they could to ensure she was okay.

"We're not charging you rent," George called from the living room next door.

Ineke whipped her attention to Greg. "Why?"

George strode in. "Because if you're working for us, rent and bills are in with the wages."

Greg gave him what Ineke thought was a 'thank you' nod. What were they playing at? She'd caught on quick that they spoke without words to one another, maybe some kind of twin telepathy, and it was still going on now; they stared at each other for quite a while until she was forced to break it.

"But I don't work for you," she said.

"You will be if you accept our offer." George leaned against the cupboard by the sink. "We need someone to invest money for us—the legitimate money. Stocks and shit. Someone who can keep an eye on it and reinvest elsewhere if it looks like we're going to lose revenue. You were studying shit like that in Amsterdam, yes? The extra cash we get from it will be used for a charity we're going to set up."

"What charity?"

"We're opening a refuge for people like you. Somewhere for them to go if they need to get away from bitches like your mother. There's this big house we've got our eye on. Should be enough to hold twenty people. Vic's going to give them therapy, then when they're strong enough, and it's safe enough for them to be out there by themselves, we'll employ them, get them into a place of their own."

It *could* be seen that this was a creepy, underhand way to get people to join their ranks, and while that was a bonus for them, Ineke didn't imagine that was the sole reason. Did she dare think her story had sparked something inside them, a need to further help others? Debbie had already told her the twins liked to make people's lives better—and in contrast, they made them worse or ended them, too. It seemed they were genuinely two of life's good people, deep down, torture and murder aside.

How can being with these people be better than at home? At least with Moeder, I knew what was coming, but this lot?

Was she right to be cautious, despite feeling as if she fitted in? Or was she so desperate to belong that she'd take anything? Even killers?

"Reckon you could do that as well as working for Debbie and doing the uni thing?" George asked. "The investing is only an hour or two every now and then."

"Yes."

"I'm not happy about you being out all night," Greg said. "So we've assigned a bodyguard to stand by the trees in Kitchen to watch over you."

"But Debbie has watchers there, she told me about them."

"Yeah, but I want one man on you specifically."

Greg stared at her so intently, she blushed. He looked good without a beard, she could see all of his face, the whole of any expressions. This one showed his concern, how much he wanted her to be safe. How much he *liked* her.

Oh God.

"You've been through a lot," he said. "And you don't have the protection you had in Amsterdam in a job like that. Are you…um, are you going to be offering your services?"

"No. Just overseeing the women."

He nodded, a small smile playing out. "Right. Good."

"Fuck me," George grumbled. "Have you two got perfume and aftershave on, or is that attraction I can smell?" He walked out.

"A bad Dad joke," Greg called after him. He shrugged at Ineke. "Ignore him. He's a dick."

"A kind dick."

"Yeah. When do you start with Debbie?"

"Tomorrow night."

"Fancy seeing the West End later? Dinner? George *won't* be coming."

"I heard that!" George shouted.

"Bugger off, you fucking earwigger." Greg shifted from foot to foot. "This is…I rarely do this. Go out with a woman. We're too busy. But I'll try to make time."

"Is it a date?" she asked.

"If you want it to be."

She nodded. "That would be nice, but I need to get something to wear." She currently had some of Debbie's clothes on.

"In the wardrobe." George appeared in the doorway. "Debbie organised for a load of stuff to be brought here." He glanced between her and Greg. "I'll get this bit over and done with, because listening to my brother bumbling is fucking painful. He likes you. He wants to see where this goes, but he doesn't want to scare you or make you feel like you have to say yes because you feel you owe us. You never have to say that anymore, understand? Your life, your thoughts, your everything are your own. And if you ever feel like he's putting pressure on you, which he won't, come and see me. I'll punch him in the face for you."

"For fuck's sake, George." Greg sighed and looked at Ineke. "Can you put up with this? Him butting in? He's a bloody nightmare."

Ineke smiled. "I can put up with it."

George winked at her. "There. Sorted. Cards on the table. How easy was that? Now, go and have a gander round the rest of the flat to see if we've forgotten anything. If we have, say so. Oh, and there's some money in an envelope on the bedside table. A gift. Buy yourself something nice." He jerked his head at Greg. "Come on, we've got to go and see Ichabod. Something came up while we were away, and it's still bugging him."

"The Laundrette Lil thing?" Greg asked.

"Yeah."

"Sorry," Greg said to Ineke. "We're like coppers, never at home. The Estate…it takes up a lot of our time."

"It is fine. Go."

The twins left. Ineke shook her head at how her fortunes had changed so quickly. Three knights without shining armour had swept in and rescued her, bringing her to the new world she'd dreamed about so often. A place where she could be herself and not think about Moeder.

If it seems too good to be true ...

"Fuck off. Just fuck off." She clenched the sides of her hair, desperate for that evil voice to go away.

Would Monster's cruel taunts always follow her? Would going to see Vic help her to cope with it? She'd be seeing him tomorrow morning at ten and had already made the decision to tell him absolutely everything. The twins had said he knew what they got up to and could be trusted with the Amsterdam story. As well as understanding Moeder and why she'd treated her the way she had, Ineke needed to understand why watching her die hadn't hurt. Most of all, she wanted to know if she was like her mother in that regard — emotionless.

She had yet to tell Christoffel, Vader, and Greet that she'd moved out of Amsterdam. She'd keep her Dutch phone only to contact them, and when the contract ran out, she'd give them the number of the new phone George had handed to her. The dust would have settled by then regarding Moeder's body being discovered.

Filled with a sense of belonging, yet strangely out on a limb in her new life, she wandered around the flat, smiling every so often, not only at the nice furniture, all those clothes and shoes and matching handbags, but the fact she'd be dating Greg. Him being called away on Estate business wouldn't bother her—she'd be so busy herself, settling into her studies and jobs. And she was used to being alone. Maybe this was for the best. Having him in her life too much would get on her nerves. Too much, too soon would only stress her.

But it could work.

Her Dutch phone bleeped, and she jumped, her stomach turning over, mouth going dry. Would it be the police? Had they found Moeder? But wouldn't they ring, not send a text? She took it out of her pocket and stared at the screen. The notification bar showed Vader had sent a message.

VADER: YOUR MOTHER HAS COMMITTED SUICIDE. I THOUGHT YOU SHOULD KNOW, EVEN THOUGH YOU TWO HAD BECOME ESTRANGED.

She stared at the words, how blunt they were, Vader's usual style even in circumstances like this. No sympathy. She supposed, if she spoke to him, he'd yet again tell her it was something she just had to get on with by herself—the grief, if she had any, would belong solely to her, but she doubted he'd feel any. She'd bet if Greet had died, he wouldn't tell Christoffel in this way, he'd sit him down and be kind, a hug on hand. Why could he show his emotions to him and Greet but not her? Ineke didn't even look like Moeder, so even that wasn't an excuse.

Because he's not your father, remember.

INEKE: IT DOESN'T SURPRISE ME. SHE'S TRIED IT BEFORE DON'T FORGET.

VADER: ONLY A MATTER OF TIME BEFORE SHE SUCCEEDED. THERE WILL BE A POST-MORTEM LATER, BUT THE POLICE FEEL IT'S CUT AND DRIED. WILL YOU BE ATTENDING THE FUNERAL?

INEKE: NO.

VADER: I DIDN'T THINK SO.

INEKE: DON'T YOU EVEN WANT TO KNOW WHY WE WERE ESTRANGED FOR THE PAST TWO YEARS?

VADER: NO.

INEKE: I KNOW WHO YOU ARE. OR WHO YOU'RE NOT.

VADER: IT HAD TO COME OUT SOMETIME.

INEKE: WHO IS MY FATHER?

VADER: I'LL SEND YOU DETAILS LATER. GOODBYE.

So he was really washing his hands of her. Really didn't care.

Am I supposed to be hurting now? I have no father, not really, and definitely no mother. Why can't I cry? Why is this all so…normal?

Another text came in.

GREET: ARE YOU OKAY? DO YOU NEED SOMEONE TO TALK TO? WHY HAVEN'T YOU BEEN AT WORK THE PAST FEW DAYS?

INEKE: I DON'T DO THAT ANYMORE.

GREET: GOOD, YOU ARE SO MUCH BETTER THAN THAT. AND UNIVERSITY? YOU HAVEN'T BEEN, I ASKED THEM. THEY SAID YOU'D LEFT. AND I WENT TO YOUR FLAT AND YOU WEREN'T THERE. A NEIGHBOUR SAID YOU'D MOVED OUT.

INEKE: I'VE STARTED AGAIN.

GREET: WHERE?

INEKE: SOMEWHERE SAFE, AWAY FROM ALL THE MEMORIES.

GREET: WHAT MEMORIES? IS THERE SOMETHING YOU NEED TO TALK ABOUT? PLEASE CONTACT ME IF YOU NEED TO. I HATE TO THINK OF YOU BEING ALONE.

INEKE: I HAVE A NEW FAMILY NOW. I'LL BE FINE.

GREET: OH. OKAY.

INEKE: AND I KNOW. ABOUT MY FATHER.

Ineke waited for more, but nothing came. Perhaps Greet had taken offence at those words — that a new family meant more than the old one. In some ways it did. Greet's caring aside, Christoffel was the only person Ineke wanted to keep in contact with, despite him not being her brother.

She'd have to let the twins know the news. She'd been told how to write things that needed to be kept secret, a code of sorts, just in case the police ever became involved and her phone was seized. She selected the joint number they used for business, adding Moon and Debbie to the chat. It could look strange, if the Dutch police poked into it, that Ineke had left Amsterdam the day after Moeder had died, and the first people she contacted about it were known leaders of London Estates and a woman who had dealings with them, but if Vader was right, nothing would come of the investigation — he may even steer it elsewhere so it didn't infect him. Judge Evi Meijer, who had kept her husband's surname (likely another way to cling to the past), had simply slit her own wrist because life had become too much — and that was all.

Maybe Vader knew, somehow, that Ineke had been involved. Maybe he'd do his best to keep her name out of it. One last pretend-father act.

INEKE: MY FATHER HAS JUST LET ME KNOW THAT MY MOTHER HAS KILLED HERSELF. THE POLICE DON'T FEEL IT'S SUSPICIOUS, AND ANYWAY, SHE'S TRIED IT BEFORE. I'M OKAY, BUT I JUST NEEDED TO TELL SOMEONE.

GG: SORRY. DO YOU WANT US TO COME AND SIT WITH YOU?

INEKE: NO, BUT THANKS FOR THE OFFER.

DEBBIE: AWW, SO SORRY, LOVE.

MOON: SENDING HUGS.

That was it. Done.

Now it was in fate's hands.

The final text she'd ever get from Vader had arrived.

VADER: BART CLASSEN.

Two words that should fill her with hope of a new beginning but instead blocked her chance of ever having a father. Bart Classen, Henrik's right-hand man, dead. The man who'd *raped* her in the hotel, a knife to her throat.

Her own father had used her.

She scrunched her eyes shut, sickened.

Her mind raced, so many questions. So he'd been an electrician in a former life? Or was that his gang name? Was Moeder telling Hendrik to approach Ineke that night a sick game she'd played, knowing her daughter's father would have a hand in killing her? She'd said she'd wanted Bart to do it—what kind of evil bitch *was* she, getting a father to kill his child? And Hendrik paying off the tuition fees, that had to be have been with Moeder's money. And the clearing of her flat—had he taken all of her things to Moeder, or had she told him to dump them?

She sank onto the sofa, shaking her head at how someone could be so cruel. Ineke may not have wanted to know a father who was a criminal, but she'd been denied the chance to choose.

Once again, Moeder had pulled the strings.

But she won't win. I won't let her.

Rijzen.

Living her best life now, smiling and happy, would have Moeder turning in her grave. Ineke would have the last laugh after all.

Chapter Twenty-Two

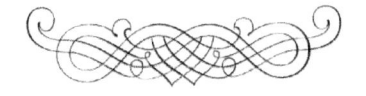

Moon had done a lot of thinking in that backstreet room and since he'd come home. Stepping off that plane onto the tarmac had given him such a whoosh of relief that he reckoned he'd never go away without Debbie again. It gave him the willies just thinking about the mess he'd got himself into. Stupid bastard, always thinking he knew best, and not even telling Debbie, the twins, Alien, or Brickhouse exactly what he was doing and who he was doing it with. Why had he done that, not covered his own back? What, did he think he was some kind of superhero who couldn't be killed? What a dick.

He grimaced at himself. If he wasn't him, and he'd seen someone behaving like he had, he'd have taken them down a peg or two, shown them the error of their ways. Hendrik had done that by locking him in that room, yet Moon suspected that had happened because the bloke hadn't known how to handle being told no. Moon had been like that once upon a time. Still was to a degree.

Fuck international relations in the criminal community; he wasn't getting into bed with any of them in the future. He'd been burned. Badly. On the flight, he'd promised himself he'd stick to London from now on—and if he had the urge to chase the highs of his youth, he'd do it with the woman he loved. Maybe they could go to Marbella or something, a long weekend of partying and having fun. They could get rat-arsed, and he could pretend he was her age, not his. But he'd seen from his hangovers in

Amsterdam that he wasn't really up to that anymore, his body protesting.

Fuck this getting old lark. No one told me my knees would grate like sandpaper.

He stared outside at people going to and fro, all busy, all with shit to do. Men waited for their women outside shops, or they walked along arm in arm, together. They were spending time with their other halves, yet what had he done?

You're a bastard.

Debbie sat opposite him, glancing around and rolling her eyes, her cheeks a little flushed. Was she angry that he'd brought her here? Had he fucked it up yet again? They sat in a posh café Up West, the necklace he'd bought this morning burning a hole in his pocket. He had to make it up to Debbie, his time away, his disregard for her, how easily he'd forgotten she'd existed while he'd indulged in trying to claw back the youth he'd once had. He didn't love her enough if he could do that, he had to try harder, do better. It was a wonder she'd still been there when he'd strolled into his house, but then Debbie knew how leaders worked, she understood she'd be second fiddle. But she shouldn't be, and he'd make that known now. He clearly hadn't learned from his mistakes with his ex-wife.

They'd had a cream tea, the remnants of it on a three-tier cake stand, the breadcrumbs the only evidence they'd had cucumber sandwiches with no crusts on. Bloody ridiculous, if you asked him, a sandwich that wasn't a hearty doorstep made with fresh crusty bread, but he'd wanted her to have the fine-dining experience, to do something special. Show her that even if this cost an arm and a leg, she was worth it.

But maybe that had been his trouble all along. Throwing gifts at her instead of giving her the greatest gift that came for free—his time.

Jesus, he was sounding like a self-help book. The twins would think he was a right old plonker. George would take the piss.

"I don't belong here," Debbie said for the umpteenth time, as if she thought it needed repeating, that he hadn't taken the hint and got her the fuck out of there.

I've missed the cues again.

She sighed. "So now we've finished, can we go?"

"Princesses belong anywhere, but I know what you mean. Sorry if bringing you here made you uncomfortable, that wasn't my intention. I'm a bit shit at all this, aren't I? I just wanted to do something nice with you."

"I appreciate that, but maybe next time take me somewhere people don't brown-nose themselves or each other. Did you hear those women at that table just now? Talk about believing their own hype."

Like I did. Like Hendrik. He winced in shame. "Hmm."

"Are you all right?" she asked.

So she'd picked up on his discomfort straight away. He ought to be ashamed of himself for not giving her the same courtesy. He took her arm and guided her outside, down the busy street with more brown-nosers, all dressed as if they'd strolled out of the clothing section in Harrods. He had to admit, he didn't belong here either. He was too brash, too common.

So why bring her here, then? She'd have preferred a greasy café with pie and mash, not those poncy sandwiches.

He led her down the street to an alley.

"Where are we going?" she asked.

"Thought it would be nice to walk in the park."

"Moon, it's fucking *freezing*, not to mention it's going to piss down in a minute and I didn't bring my brolly. And *you*, walk in a park? Are you off your rocker?"

"I don't often tell you to shut up, but shut up, Deb."

She glared at him. "I can't believe you just said that. You cheeky fucking bastard! You—"

"Listen," he said as they emerged from the alley into a large green area with gravel pathways, a bandstand in the distance beside a lake, kids running around like loons. "I've got to get something off my chest. I need to apologise for the way I am sometimes. I get so caught up in business and lose sight of what's most important. That's you, by the way. I was locked in that room, and I thought: What the fuck are you playing at, mate? You've got Debbie at home, and here you are, fucking about abroad."

"It was business, so I get it, although you *were* gone for a long time."

"Yeah, but business wasn't smoking weed and getting off my face. Anything could have happened and I wouldn't have known, I was too out of it. I was chasing the old days, fucking selfish bastard, part of me paranoid life was going by so quickly instead of enjoying it with you at the new pace. I'm getting on a bit, no idea why you're with an old fart like me, and I forgot you were at home, waiting. I *forgot*, Deb, and I shouldn't have. So I wanted to say sorry, for everything, and can we start again?"

"You sound like I've given you some kind of ultimatum when I haven't. You do you, I do me, that's how it's always been between us. I like it that way. I thought you did, too."

"Yeah, but I need to pay you more attention. Come on, half the time you're rattling around that house while I'm off overseeing murder and all the other shit I get up to."

She stopped walking. Stared at him. "I also have my business to run. I don't sit there pining for you, you know. Well, maybe a bit, but whatever. And are you about to tell me you're going to retire? Because one, you'd be bored shitless and drive me up the wall, and two, you've got so much more to give your Estate. Don't get all jealous, but Alien and Brickhouse coped fine without you, so maybe think about letting them continue that and you get involved in other projects. Like what George and Greg are doing with the refuge. Make your money work for others instead of it just sitting there. Do something significant with it. I'll help you, if you like, then we can be together more if that's what you're after, but I'm warning you, as soon as you get on my nellies, I'll tell you."

He chuckled at 'nellies'. At how she was so perfect for him. She gave him space, understood his needs. "You're a good woman, Deb."

"I know."

He took the box out of his pocket and flipped the lid up. "I got you something."

"As saying sorry goes, this is exactly what I'd expect from you, and at least it isn't a bunch of petrol station flowers." She smiled. She prodded him in the chest. "Put it on me then!"

He fumbled the necklace and dropped it on the grass. Bent to pick it up, cursing himself for being a clumsy cunt, how she should be with someone with a bit of finesse about them instead of him, someone who paid her attention. He draped the diamonds around her neck, a memory intruding of the time he'd done this with his ex, the mother of his kids. Seemed he'd always bought apologies.

He glanced to the sky and hoped his dead daughter looked down, happy for him. He'd led a good life in some respects, but in others he'd been heartbroken, broken in general. Lumbering around in anger, breaking others so they'd feel as shitty as he had. But Debbie had fixed all that.

"I fucking love you," he said, a lump in his throat, and he did up the clasp. "I mean proper love you."

"I proper love you, too." She turned and laid her hands on his shoulders. "And whatever you need forgiven, it's done. Forgotten. New start. But whatever you do, just don't get under my feet, all right? And don't expect me to give up my shit to follow you round. I've got women to look after, and I won't give that up."

"I'd never expect you to."

He took her arm again and slipped the box in his pocket. She was a good sort, his Debbie, one of the best. He'd been a fool to take her for granted. Tomorrow, he was changing his will and adding her to his life insurance payout. She had money of her own, but he wanted to make sure she was all right when he was gone. Almost being killed—because Hendrik would have ordered that if he hadn't agreed to take the women—had brought a few things home. That he wasn't invincible, he'd die one day, the only bonus getting to see his little girl again, hopefully, if Heaven existed. But for now, he'd do what Debbie said, get a new purpose. Do something good.

And maybe it would make up for all the bad.

Fuck me, you've gone soft in your old age.

But maybe that was what love did. Softened you.

Chapter Twenty-Three

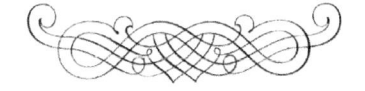

In the office at Jackpot Palace, Ichabod sat behind the desk, George and Greg opposite. They'd had a quick squiz at the takings and a chat about how Rowan was settling in now he was taking on the bulk of the managerial tasks for when they needed to whisk Ichabod away on other jobs, but it was about time they got down to whatever was going on.

A woman who managed one of their earlier business fronts seemed to think two people who'd come in to wash quilts in the larger machines were plotting to kill someone. It should sound shocking, but it didn't. People talked about murder a lot around here, mainly in jest, but the few times it was serious, well, it was best to nip it in the bud.

It comes to something when murder is normal.

"So you reckon it has legs?" George asked Ichabod. "This, whatever it is."

"Ye'd be better off speakin' tae Lil yeself, see what ye make of her story. I don't know her enough tae gauge whether she's makin' a mountain out of a molehill, but it's been botherin' me for days, so it has. She wouldn't tell me exactly what was said, reckons she needs tae tell ye two the ins and outs. I said ye'd be back shortly, that ye'd gone for a little holiday up north—I thought that was better, because again, I don't know whether she's the type tae go blabbin' about ye not bein' in the country. All sorts could have gone on if the residents knew, and I'm nowhere near up tae scratch to cope wid anything on the same level as ye do."

George nodded. "You did the right thing. How did she know to get hold of you?"

"I heard from Martin, who'd been past that way collectin' protection money. She'd come out and asked him why no messages she'd sent ye had been answered. He got hold of me—I assume ye told him tae do that if I was needed—and I went round there."

"Hmm, she did send quite a few texts, but we didn't get back to her because she sent another one saying you were dealing with it." George sighed. "So what's the score now?"

"She told me the people had arranged tae go back the same time this Friday night. Want me tae go and have a listen?"

"Please. Pose as someone doing their washing. Anything from the laundrette CCTV?"

"They had their heads down, but they're women, both blonde."

"Did you contact Bennett about outside?"

He was their CCTV man, along with a reluctant new recruit, Jones, a bloke frightened into being part of their team. Both worked shifts, manning street cameras and reporting anything iffy to the police—and to the twins as a side hustle, not that they had any choice in the matter. Their patch happened to cover the laundrette.

"Yeah. He got the relevant files up and followed their route after they left the laundrette. He lost them at the junction by the Noodle."

George had chosen to buy the Tiger and Noodle pub in that location specifically *because* there were no cameras. It had gone against them here, but so long as the women returned to the laundrette on Friday, it didn't matter. Ichabod was a professional when it came to surveillance, and he'd soon find out who they were and where they lived. Failing that, Nessa, their manager, might be able to help.

"So maybe they live around there," Greg said. "We might know them if they drink in the pub, or Nessa will."

"I just thought the same," George said. "But we don't know what they look like, so we're up shit creek."

"He sent me some stills of them." Ichabod got his phone out. "Want me tae forward them tae ye?"

"Please." George waited for them to come through and had a gander. "They could be anyone. But at least we know one's got long hair, the other short, and they're both skinny." He stood. "We'll nip and see Lil, then we need to see if Mason's come up with anything about Bryan Flint. Last I heard he was gathering intel."

"Such a pisser that Janine won't be wid us for much longer," Ichabod said, standing. "It's grand that she's startin' a family, though. It might calm her the feck down."

"Hmm, can't see that happening. Janine's a law unto herself. How's Marleigh?"

Ichabod walked round the desk to the door, his hand perched on the knob. "She's all right. We're keepin' a low profile until everythin' has died down, as agreed. Her mammy's there a lot, though, so I have tae message tae make sure the coast is clear before I go round, otherwise she'll rip Marleigh a new one about seein' a man so close to David dyin'."

"Getting along all right, though?"

"As well as we can when her husband's death is hangin' over us. Yeah, she knew it would happen, but it doesn't mean it hasn't left a scar. The feckin' bastard still has the ability tae rile me up, even though he's dead. Marleigh's strugglin' tae deal wid her part in it—not that she'd grass us up, just the fact he lied tae her, havin' that other woman and kid behind her back, and she wanted tae make him pay. She thinks that means she's a bad person, but I keep tellin' her everyone has dark thoughts."

"Understandable, poor cow." Greg rose and straightened his suit jacket. "Let's get things sorted. I've got a date tonight and don't want to make a bad impression by being late."

"A date?" Ichabod opened the door and walked into the corridor. "That's not like ye."

"Yeah, well, people change. Life changes you." Greg smiled. "She's the woman we brought back from Amsterdam."

"Ah, it'll be nice for ye tae have some normality. I didn't realise how much I needed somethin' like that until now. All work and no play… It's just ye next, George, then we'll all have someone."

"Fuck that. After Janet, I've been put off for life."

They laughed all the way into the casino, but George didn't find it funny. He was destined to be alone for the rest of his life because of her.

Chapter Twenty-Four

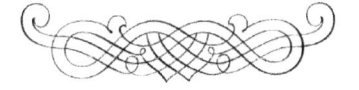

Lil's Laundrette had belonged to Lil herself once upon a time until the twins had muscled in and offered her a deal she couldn't turn down, resulting in her selling it to them. They were good at that, taking over, and had a fair few businesses now. No one else knew they owned them, and Lil had lied her arse off to nosy customers when the new machines had replaced the old, the place getting a nice little makeover—"Got a loan, didn't I, and what the fuck's it got to do with you, nose-ache?" All she had to do was oversee the service washes in the evenings these days, and another woman, Maria, ran it during the day where dry-cleaning was available, too. Her daughter, Cassidy, and some other bird were also daytime employees.

George had secured a client who ran a hotel down the road, telling him he'd be much better off having his sheets and whatnot done at Lil's, and the profits had shot up, what with B&Bs in the area all taking his words of advice: basically go to Lil's or we'll have something to say about it—"Oh, and you'll have to pay us protection money, too."

This meant the back of the laundrette, previously unused and a waste of space gathering dust, had been kitted out to accommodate all that was needed to wash and iron sheets. The large press made short work of the job, and the place smelled lovely every time George walked in. Cleanliness, a mix of Daz, Ariel, and Lenor, all sorts. It reminded him of his mother's wash days. A comfort.

They rarely had to come here for business, although this was where Greg took a lot of their suits to be cleaned. Lil had it all in hand, no need to badger them about this and that, and for her to think something was up meant it likely was. Ichabod didn't know her, didn't realise that if Lil had made contact it was serious. She wasn't one for blowing smoke up anyone's arse and preferred to fix things on her own.

Evidently, there wasn't enough glue to fix this issue.

George pushed the door open and took a deep breath. He'd messaged Lil to get her arse round to the laundrette so they could have a chat in the small staffroom. She valued her privacy and didn't want them round her place, never had, and they didn't want her round theirs. Although he'd bet they'd see Ineke there before long, staying over, her laughter brightening up the place. If she had it in her to laugh. But one day, soon.

He inhaled, got his dose of my-eyes-are-stinging memories, then approached the counter, Greg giving him a small smile as he inhaled, too.

"All right, Maria?" George asked.

She smiled, her cheeks ruddy from the heat. Wisps of brown hair had attached themselves to her face. She was only in her mid-thirties but appeared older. Worn out. Her old man had fucked off when their daughter had been born, and she'd struggled ever since.

"Yes, thank you, Mr Wilkes. You?"

"Fine as it goes. Is Lil here yet?"

Maria nodded. "She's out the back." She lifted a portion of the counter for them to pop through. "Everything all right?"

"Your job's safe if that's what you're fishing for." George nosed through the indoor window into the dry-cleaning area. "Blimey, your Cassidy's grown."

Maria's face lit up. "She turned eighteen last Wednesday. We had a party at the weekend. You were invited but never answered my message — just wanted to get that out there in case you took offence and thought we didn't ask you."

"We were a bit tired, and come on, she wouldn't have wanted us there cramping her style."

And we don't have to answer to you. If we don't want to go to a party, we don't fucking go.

Jesus, I need to get some proper sleep. Moody bastard.

Guilt took hold. It wasn't her fault he'd been burning the candle at both ends. He took one of his usual envelopes from his jacket pocket, ones he ensured were there so he could help people if he bumped into them. "I'll give her a little present."

Maria's eyebrows hiked up. "That's very kind of you."

"Yeah, I can be sometimes." He pushed the door and stepped into the other room, Greg behind him. "I hear someone got the key to adulthood."

Cassidy, dyed black hair all over the place, her mascara streaked from the steam, paused what she was doing. "I did. Doesn't make Mum stop treating me like a kid, though. When do they let you grow up, eh?"

"Be grateful you've got a mother who gives a shit," Greg said, a tad testily.

Cassidy picked up on the tension and gave them a lopsided smile. "I love her, I just don't need her in my ear all the time, that's all. Have you come to collect some washing? I don't recall seeing any of your suits…"

"Nah, we're here to see Lil." George placed the envelope on the side. "Birthday present from us."

She peered inside. "Bloody hell!"

George smiled. "Treat yourself."

"Maybe buy your mum some flowers an' all," Greg said. "Some people don't have anyone like Maria in their lives."

George stared at him. "All right, she gets the message." He walked into the staffroom, a genuine smile splitting his lips apart. "Fuck my old boots, Lil. What are you like?"

"You should know by now," she said. "We've known each other long enough."

Greg came in and shut the door. "Jesus…this is a step up from the usual getup."

Fifty-two-year-old Laundrette Lil sat on a brown leather sofa, neck to ankle in a leopard-print catsuit. Her hair, a bright-pink wig today, coiled in some kind of up-do, clashed with her dark eyebrows which she'd drawn on. Eye shadow, the colours belonging on an acid trip, created a rainbow, and thick mascara—or was that fake lashes?—meant she'd been interrupted in her charity work and hadn't had time to tone it down for this chat.

She visited Elm House, the local care home, during the day, singing karaoke and generally brightening the old dodgers' days—her mother had been in hospice there at the end, and Lil wanted to give back, to do something worth doing. A heart of gold sat in her abundant chest, and she was one of those rare people who got you smiling, even when you didn't want to. But she also had a bad habit of overstepping the mark, saying it how it was, blunt like George. He hoped she wasn't in one of those moods today because he couldn't be doing with it.

Her usual smile wasn't present now, though.

Fuck, here we go…

She glared at them. "Since when did you two not answer your phone?"

George sat at the small table. "Since when do you get to have a go at us about it?"

"I wasn't having a go, merely mentioning it." She scoffed at the scowl he pointed in her direction. "Anyway, I'm that annoyed. The one time I need you, and you weren't available. Sod's law."

"Ichabod was here to cover us." Greg flicked the kettle on and took cups out of a wall cupboard.

"But *I* didn't know that, did I, not until he said."

"We don't have to explain ourselves to anyone, Lil." George parted his knees and draped his clasped hands between them. She was a good sort, but fucking hell, he had to stop himself from getting up and grabbing her, barking in her face to mind her manners.

"I suppose." She folded her arms. "Mine's a coffee," she said to Greg. "Two sugars, no milk. Cheers."

Greg slanted the evil eye her way, but it seemed to fly right over her head. That or she was making out she hadn't seen it.

"Tell us what went on." George stared at the floor rather than at her. If she dished out one more scathing remark, he might say something to her, then she'd regret ever opening her mouth. And he'd regret opening his. Lil was harmless, if a bit of a bossy cow, and he had to remember that. It was just her way.

"Well," she said. "These two women came in. Twenties, the end nearer to thirty, blonde, skinny. They lugged in these black bags and took quilts out. Fair enough, I thought, that's what goes on here, you wash your duvets, but they took them out of brand-new packets, so that was the first thing I thought was fucking weird. So of *course* I was going to listen. One of them, she says, 'We have to make sure we do this right. One, we don't want the police to come knocking, and two, if The Brothers find out…' Well, I said to myself they were up to no good, didn't I, and when one of them turned my way, but only to the side so I couldn't see her properly, I put my earbuds in to make out I wasn't listening. I even went so far as to fiddle with my phone like I was putting music on. But did I fuck."

"Right…"

"So the one who looked at me, she faced the front again. I didn't have my long-distance glasses on, bloody left them at home, which was a bugger, otherwise I'd have been able to see them in the reflection in the window. Anyway, she says, 'If we stab him, it'll look more plausible.' What's that supposed to mean? And the other one, she says, 'But we'll get blood on us.' Now, as you can imagine, that piqued my interest. Has it piqued yours? Because it bloody should do. An upcoming murder on your turf? One they don't want you to know about? Bastard liberty."

"Yep, we're interested." George always found he lost himself whenever Lil told a story—lost himself to the past, the memories. This was how Mum and her best mate used to chatter, all this "Well, and *then* she said..." business going on. He'd had to remind himself to take in all of Lil's words, to remain in the present.

Sometimes, missing Mum was a proper ache in his chest.

Greg handed out the drinks then sat opposite George. "Sounds to me like these women either need a hand in bumping someone off—us doing it for them—or someone needs protecting from them."

Lil got off the sofa and joined them at the table, a waft of perfume filling the air. "Exactly what I thought. But which way round is it?"

George couldn't work out whether he liked her scent or not, then decided he didn't. Too strong. "We'll find that out. Ichabod's going to come here on Friday night, bring some washing, make out he's a customer."

"Tell him to do what I did and put earbuds in, then." Lil nodded to herself as if she was the only person on the planet to have thought of such a thing.

"He's not green," George said. "He'll even be in disguise. Now there's a thing!"

"Sarcasm is the lowest form of wit, George." Lil drew her cup towards her and pursed her red lips. "But what did I expect from you?"

"He'll never change," Greg said. "Which is why he'll get one of his little envelopes out and thank you for the information."

Lil laughed. "Much as that would come in handy—I've seen a nice catsuit in town I've had my eye on—we all know that's part of my job, grassing, which I already get paid for."

"Yeah, well, it doesn't hurt to get a bonus." Greg sipped his coffee and stared across the table.

George took an envelope out, staring right back. "I was going to do it anyway. I don't need prompting. Fuck me." He pushed it towards her. "Thank you for the information." He threw a dirty look at Greg then smiled at Lil. "Have you seen the women before?"

Lil rolled her eyes. "Weren't you *listening*? I couldn't see their faces."

"Sorry, must have missed that bit." He hadn't. "I just wanted to check if anything else had stood out, that's all."

"Only that one looked skint, too thin, which didn't add up if they had new quilts. But there *was* something else they said, after they'd talked about the stabbing. I don't know if it'll be relevant, though."

"We'll decide that." George wished he had a custard cream to dip into his drink. It would go with the abundance of memories he'd been smacked with since he'd entered the laundrette. "Spit it out."

"One of them said he'd changed his women, that he'd moved on to Kitchen Street. I assumed he uses prossers."

"Sex workers," Greg corrected and sent daggers her way.

Lil's eyes widened, and she poked the tabletop with her long scarlet nail. "Listen here, you, it's one thing for me to do what you want, be your ears an' all that, but don't tell me what words I can use. I'm fifty-two and don't intend to change, even if you get snarky with me. You boys don't scare me, remember that."

"It's a sore subject with him at the moment," George said.

"What, prossers?" Lil eyed Greg sagely. "'Ere, you haven't got yourself one of them STDs off a tart, have you? I thought you didn't have anything to do with women?"

"No, nothing like that."

"Some say you're bent. Gay."

Greg stared over at George: *I'm out of this one. You deal with it before I lose my shit.*

George sighed. "Whether he's gay or not shouldn't have to be announced. He isn't, but that's not the point. Also, it's none of your fucking business, and if you hear anyone else talking about him, tell them that."

"Keep your ruddy hair on! I was only passing on the gossip like you *pay* me to. God, damned if you do and damned if you don't."

"Let's move on before I bite your head off. You're winding me up." George drank some coffee. "Anything else we might need to know?"

"Just that one has a kid, a little boy. Think she called him Delaney or some such fancy bollocks. So that's about the long and short of it. They sat there without talking for the whole time the duvets finished washing, *and* when they were drying—another weird thing if you ask me. I took it that they aren't mates. They'd have been nattering if they were."

"So they could just be two women who know each other through him? The bloke they want to stab?"

Lil shrugged. "Could be. Your guess is as good as mine."

"Cheers, we'll take it from here."

"If they come in before Friday, I'll let you know. I'll get Maria to keep an eye out for two blondes." Lil tapped the table. "Those quilts being in the packet is still bothering me. Why wash new ones?"

"Fuck knows, but maybe we'll find out."

Chapter Twenty-Five

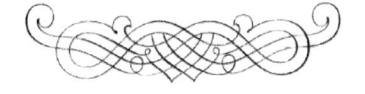

Mason had come through with the information. Bryan Flint was safe to approach, dodgy as fuck but not necessarily willing to walk over to the dark side—or the darker side. Word on the street was that he took bribes from criminals, so he was already cloaked in black, but running his own scam on the side was completely different to going in with the twins and being told what to do. Maybe he'd buck against that, wouldn't like taking orders, but Janine wanted a new man on the block as soon as possible to reduce her stress, so the bloke would just have to lump it. Mason had been following him and now had some audio that had been interesting listening.

Armed with the evidence that would ensure Flint agreed to be their piece of filth—with a little persuasion—George and Greg made their way to the King's Arms where the copper currently sat nursing a beer, off-duty. Mason was also in there, keeping an eye on him.

"What are we going to do if he turns us down?" Greg asked from the passenger seat of their BMW. "Just so I know and can prepare myself."

"The warehouse. We can't risk him flapping his gums to his seniors, so if it looks like he will, we get rid."

Greg sighed. "I had a feeling you'd say that. Topping a copper is risky. They go all in when it's one of their own. Try harder to find the killer."

"Yep, but rather that than us being questioned for trying to turn him. Anyway, with a few words in the right ears via Janine, him going missing could be put down to some crims doing him over."

"Janine can't afford to be dropping that kind of information anymore. We agreed, what with the vigilante angle getting a bit hairy, she should keep her head down when it comes to suggesting shit to her colleagues."

"Yeah, but if she puts it in a way where's she's shooting the breeze, nattering to a coworker about something she overheard, it should be okay."

Greg reached for a lemon sherbet from the glove box, opened it, and put it in George's mouth. "Are you sure we've got enough on him?"

George tucked the sweet into his cheek. "Don't you? Fucking hell, how much do we need?"

"Fair enough. He's definitely a wrong 'un."

"A lot of people are."

George drove in silence for a while, thinking about Ineke's mother being found—it wasn't exactly something he could forget, considering it could land them right in the shite. *Would* it be swept under the rug as a suicide? Or would some jobsworth pathologist notice the wrist slash wasn't *quite* how the woman would have done it?

He comforted himself that with thousands of people visiting Amsterdam at one time, they wouldn't suspect a tourist, would they? They wouldn't check all flights into the city and spot their names in the log, would they? Ineke had said her mother had tried it before, so was that on record? He hoped it was, because it would point the police in that direction nicely.

Hendrik and his men. Would that scrote moped kid create merry hell if he couldn't get hold of any of them? If he was a drug dealer and relied on that to earn a crust, he'd be desperate if he wasn't given more or Hendrik didn't answer his calls. Greg had made out he'd had gone to Russia, so it would buy some time, but…

Don't think about it until you have to.

"You take the lead when we get there," Greg said.

George laughed. "I already planned to. Your mind's filled with Ineke, so you won't be much cop."

"Hmm."

"Could be dangerous, letting yourself get involved when her mum's just snuffed it—the link between you could look suss. And just remember who we are, what we do. Our heads need to be in the game at work, so you need to forget about her while you're on the job. After hours, as well as your head, she can fill whatever she likes."

"Don't even go there with an innuendo about me filling her."

"I wasn't going to!"

"Bollocks."

George chuckled. "You've got to admit, it would have been a funny joke."

"Not with this one. Not with her."

Fuck, he's got it bad.

Greg stared out of the window, a finger across his chin. "Don't take the piss out of me, but she could be the one."

George held back his need to laugh and poke fun. Now wasn't the time to prod the bear. He was chuffed with himself for recognising that. "Don't tell me you believe in love at first sight, because you've not long met her."

"No, but when I saw her, everything else went out of the window. It shit the life out of me. You see it on the telly, but I didn't expect it to happen to me."

"Are you sure it isn't just lust? I mean, she's a pretty woman."

"No, it's more than that."

Bloody hell. "Just be careful, all right?"

"What with?"

"I'm going to sound soppy, and fuck knows I wouldn't want anyone but you to hear me say this shit, but your heart, you need to watch it. She's a good girl, but I'd hate to see you get hurt."

"How?"

"She might seem okay, but what if she's fucked in the head from her childhood? You said yourself she's just found out her dad isn't her dad. Look how we were when it happened to us."

Talking of women being fucked in the head… George thought of Janet, how easily things could have gone the other way. Love, kids, a dog. If she hadn't been a raving nutter beneath that façade of hers, he might well be living a different life by now. Maybe in that dream cottage he and Greg used to fantasise about when they were kids. Somewhere safe where the world couldn't touch them. Because if he'd truly loved Janet, he'd have wanted to protect her and any kids they had. But he'd realised, just in time, he *hadn't* loved her. Not like he should. Not like she'd wanted him to — as a version of him she felt was acceptable.

"Janet was unhinged under the surface. And don't let Ineke change you—you saw what Janet tried to do to me." George sighed. "I'm not trying to be negative here, even though you'll think I am, but I've got *your* head on for a second, the one where you're all sensible and look at both sides."

"Go on…"

"Sometimes these things are a flash in the pan. Bear that in mind."

"I will, and I've thought the same myself, which is why I'm not going to jump into bed with her. If this is real, something special, then I'm going to grow it."

"Grow it?" George snorted. "She's not a fucking plant!"

"You know what I mean, dickhead." Greg let out a huff of breath. Kept staring out of the window, as if he wanted to say more but didn't dare.

George tutted. "If you've got something on your mind, just say it. I'm your brother, you can tell me anything."

Greg's cheeks inflated with his exhale. "All right. You're not shitty about it, are you? Like I was when you went out with Janet?"

"What, all jealous because you were left on your own a few nights a week, poor boy?"

"Fuck off, I explained it wasn't just that. Something about her had always rubbed me up the wrong way. So have you got a problem, with Ineke?"

"Other than what I've already said about her possibly being fucked up, no. Oddly, it's the opposite. I want you to be happy, and if having a bird does that, then it's all good." Another flash of Greg being shot crowded George's mind. If he was fanciful, he'd say Mum had put it there to remind him that they should grab happiness while they could. They lived a dangerous life that could be ended so quickly.

Greg sighed. "You're thinking of me being shot again, aren't you. What I might not have had."

"Yep."

"Good, because maybe it means those thoughts can extend to you. You can find someone, too. Life isn't just about the Estate, bruv, about being top dog. There's so much more out there, we just haven't let ourselves go out and get it."

"I know, but who'd have me?"

"Lil for one."

"Aww, fuck right off. Can you see me mincing about with some woman in a leopard-print catsuit? Knob off, she's way too old for me."

Greg's laughter filled the car.

George smiled, just listening to it, loving it. Because once upon a time, he'd never thought he'd hear it again except in his head.

You fall in love, bruv. You deserve it. Every little thing. But if she hurts you, no matter what she's been through…

I'll fucking kill her.

Chapter Twenty-Six

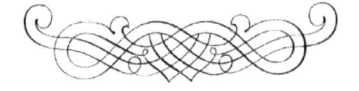

Bryan Flint had cottoned on pretty quickly that a man watched him. All right, the bloke was good, he didn't do it overtly, but being a copper, Bryan knew what signs to look out for. Since last night, he'd wondered whether one of his unofficial informants had grassed on him to his DCI, naffed off by something Bryan had said. Maybe he shouldn't have pushed him so far, too fast, but he'd had a few beers, and that was never a good thing if he wanted to keep his wits about him. How many times had he told himself not to approach people while under the influence? Why did he never listen to his own advice? He'd spent the night tossing and turning, going over and over the altercation, and he wouldn't blame the lad if he went running to the boss.

He was supposed to have all of his informants registered on file, but not everyone was prepared to have their name where other officers could see it. Some of these plebs wanted to be incognito — whether that was because they didn't want the hassle of conforming to police rules or that they enjoyed being secretive, Bryan didn't know, but it served him well to have scrotes willing to do his bidding. He didn't want their names on file either. He preferred to pocket their money for steering things in different directions for them, fucking about with reports and statements. Making things go away. Then there was that kid from last night, because that's what he was, who'd thought he was a hotshot dealer just because he ran a lucrative drug line, other little wankers his minions, but get one of them on their own, and they pissed their pants along with the best of them.

Bryan was dabbling in murky waters by fucking about with them, especially because not only did he have to be careful because he was a copper, and there was an active case on the go to find whoever ran that line, but the kids worked on Cardigan. Without permission. Just by knowing about it, as a resident, Bryan was supposed to tip The Brothers off (that unspoken rule that really got his goat), but that would mean losing out on cash. Sod that.

He glanced around, enjoying his day off. He was off tomorrow an' all and should really catch up on some sleep. Was that bloke at the bar someone involved with the drug-line kids, someone they'd badgered into scaring him off for them—or was he from work? Despite the station being large and filled with umpteen employees, Bryan still reckoned he'd recognise anyone from there, but he hadn't seen this fella before. Maybe someone based at another station had been brought in to observe him. Whatever it was, he'd have to stay alert. He couldn't risk losing his job. Getting caught. The extra money he made by pressuring his contacts came in handy. He'd got used to it. Used to the nice clothes, having the heating on without worrying about the size of the bill, buying whatever the fuck he wanted in the supermarket, and dining out.

What if I'm being followed because of the other thing, though?

Uneasy, because he was fucked if he wanted to get sent down for *that*, he sipped his pint and considered getting a bit of food. He browsed the menu, which would also serve to make the bloke think he hadn't clocked him—or that he wasn't bothered even if he had. Being a police officer had given him a level of self-assuredness he'd never had growing up. He was important now, he did a good job (if you didn't count the behind-the-scenes shit he got up to), and he fitted. His close colleagues in his team thought he was a top bloke, always there to lend a hand, nothing was ever too much trouble, although there were a couple of people in other teams he hadn't won over. One woman DI in particular always gave him shifty looks, her from the murder squad, but then she was a moody cow and did that to everyone. What was her name? Jane? Something like that. But playing the game, being nice, that was what you had to do when you were someone like him, covering your arse so if any allegations came your way, no one would believe it.

But what if someone did?

He held the menu up, keeping his gaze on the words, but in his top peripheral, he scoped his watcher out. He'd call him Nosy Parker, seeing as he was nosing. Average, that's all he was, nothing to write home about. Brown hair, a beard—or that could be a disguise—and blue eyes. Jeans, a jacket with elbow patches.

He didn't bother ordering. Something else caught his attention. The Brothers had just walked in, going to the bar and standing near Nosy Parker. Did they know him? It seemed not, because they didn't speak to each other. Nosy Parker was too busy on his phone now. Maybe sending a message about the twins? Or was this all in Bryan's imagination?

Putting his theory to the test, he left the pub and headed for his street down a road farther along. He swung his arms by his sides—keeping them in his pockets wasn't wise if he needed one of them to give someone a good clout, although punching a Brother wasn't on his to-do list, but if push came to shove and he had to defend himself, he'd do it. The footsteps behind him said *someone* followed and, rather than act a tool and look over his shoulder as if he was scared, he continued on.

At the corner of his street, he slowed but carried on walking. To get to the communal door of his small block of flats, he had to dip down a path on the left, grass and bushes either side. The door stood beneath an overhanging flat porch roof, held up by what might be classed as Greek gables but weren't as fancy as that. He reached it, put in his access code on the keypad, and stepped inside, those footsteps still close by. Just as the door started swinging shut with its usual creak, a voice halted him halfway towards the lift.

"Oi. We want a word with you."

He turned. The Brothers and Nosy Parker stared at him, all in a row blocking the exit, the door propped open with a foot. The twins came in one at a time, advancing, and Nosy Parker remained outside. A lookout?

"What do you want?" Bryan asked.

"You," one of the identikits said—there were plenty of files at the police station with variations of *that* face.

"For...?" Fuck, had they got wind of that thing, the *really bad* thing? The one that could get him banged up for years? Was it something they felt he should be punished for? It was likely.

"We've got a proposition for you."

Oh. He hadn't expected that.

Bryan backed up and leaned on the wall beside the lift doors. Folded his arms. He had to assert his authority here, even though he had none, not really. "Before we go any further, I need to tell you I'm a copper, so if you were going to say something…iffy, then don't."

"It's *because* you're a copper that we want to talk to you."

Bryan's stomach flipped. "Who sent you?"

"No one. We pick who we think is suitable after sufficient checks."

Suitable? What for? "That bloke out there, he's been watching me. Who is he?"

"Our private investigator."

What the fucking hell was going on here? Was this a trick? Had the police gone one step further in trapping people into confessions by bringing The Brothers into it, some kind of mad allegiance with Estate leaders? No, they wouldn't. Seriously? Or—and they were bound to already have a copper—had they sent the twins in to sort him out because of him being on the take? Was it that fucking DI woman? Was that why she'd been giving him filthies? Did *she* want his portion of the pie? Only a bent copper would recognise the same in another.

Jane was dodgy? No, Janine, that was it.

Calm down. "Unless you're reporting a crime, we have nothing to talk about. I'm off-duty." He pushed off the wall, put his back to them, and jabbed the lift button.

"See, that's where you're wrong."

He tensed, waiting for a smack on the head or something, but instead, his own voice filled the lobby, tinny.

"If you don't give me five hundred quid, I'll nick you, get you sent down for a fucking long stretch because we both know exactly what you're up to."

"I haven't got five hundred on me!"

"A hundred a week will do, but remember, if you don't give it to me, you're fucked, got it?"

"Okay, okay!"

"Hand the first instalment over, then."

The shuffling of money.

Shit, he knew exactly when this had happened. Last night. That bastard PI must have been tailing him, recording it. Bryan had had a pint or four so hadn't been as sharp as he usually was when dealing with the kids he bribed. Bollocks, he'd clearly missed being followed.

"Is this some bullshit trap?" Bryan asked, not daring to face them yet. Did they know about the lad running the county drug line? They must do, otherwise they wouldn't be here. Were they about to ream him a new arsehole because he hadn't told them?

Why should I? It's a police matter, sod all to do with them.

"Nope, insurance, along with some more we'll get in the future to make sure you do as you're told."

"What is it, me taking money off crims, is it against your laws? Is it only you two who can go around shafting people for protection money? I'll pack it in if it means getting you off my back."

"But if you pack it in, you won't be able to take money off *us*, will you? *We're* crims."

Bryan's heartbeat thudded so hard he felt sick. "W-what…what are you after?"

"We're in need of a full-time copper."

Oh God. Fuck, no. No! That was going a step too far, even for him. "I'm not any good at that sort of thing. You're better off finding someone else."

"From what we've heard on that audio, you're excellent at it. Turn round, you fucking ponce, the back of your head isn't attractive."

Bryan did as he was told, bricking it. Yes, he earned money on the side, but it was on his terms. This...what they were proposing... Jesus wept.

The lift door opened, dinging behind him.

He took a step back. "I swear, I'm not the right man for the job."

"We've been told you are, sunshine." The twin smiled. "I'm George, by the way. Nice to meet you. We're going to be seeing a lot of each other in future. Now then, are you going to invite us up to your gaff or let that bastard door keep butting into your leg because it can't close? It's getting right on my wick."

"I..."

"You belong to us, my old son. Now be a good boy and move out of the fucking way."

Bryan stumbled back into the lift, the two man mountains squeezing in after him.

"Don't worry, we'll teach you as we go along." George nudged him in the side as the doors closed, shutting Nosy Parker out. "But first, we've got a few things to discuss."

Chapter Twenty-Seven

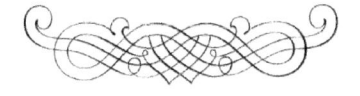

Lil stood behind the counter in the empty laundrette, eyeing the bloke who'd just come in. If this was Ichabod, he looked different to when she'd last seen him. Then, he'd had a snazzy suit on, nice shiny shoes, expensive, and his hair had been neat and tidy. Now, he was a scruffy bastard and no mistake, his clothes dirty, his hair lank. He sported a long beard that reached his chest—a bundle of pubes, that's what she thought of beards, that and the fact they hid a man's full expression. She preferred to see the whole face so she knew who she was dealing with.

Mind you, even a clean-shaven bastard can lie and you can't see it even if he hasn't got hair all over his mush.

She had some stories she could tell but preferred to keep them to herself. God, the days when she'd been a Treacle, one of Ron Cardigan's favourites. The things she'd got up to. The things he'd taught her.

Ichabod stuffed a wash load in a machine and looked over at her. "If I have tae leave before this is done…"

"I'll sort it, make sure you get it," she said. "Now don't speak to me again. And put earbuds in like I have. God, you're a useless detective."

He sat, ignoring her, and took his phone out. She'd remembered her long-distance glasses this evening and made out a game on the screen. On hers, she had Facebook, where she'd been catching up with the local gossip, then diving into strangers' feeds, friends of friends or however the fuck it worked, adding a comment here and there to wind the masses up. She'd likely be thought of as a troll, but she didn't give a shit.

Ten minutes later, the door opened, the bell above it tinkling. Lil glanced up, as she usually would, then went back to browsing, although she turned her back to lean it on the counter and watch the proceedings in the internal window. As it was dark in the dry-cleaning room beyond, this was like watching the telly.

The women, both holding black bags, used one machine between them, probably because they didn't have that much washing. So this was a mutual meeting place, nothing more.

Laundry on, they sat.

"Will he be there tomorrow night, like you thought?" Long Hair asked.

"Yes."

"Did you buy the…" Long nosed at Ichabod. "The thing?"

"Yes. I didn't open it, though. I'm not touching it without gloves on. Obviously. I got a babysitter. Mum's having Delaney. She's round mine now. He's in bed, and she thinks I've come here because my machine's broken."

"I hope she doesn't fuck about with it and sees you're lying." Long sighed. "We can do without the hassle."

"I took the fuse out of the plug. She won't pull the machine out to get to it."

"Right. We should…talk through everything, but…" Long jerked her head at Ichabod.

"Hmm."

"Okay, so we'll meet at half past seven at The Angel, then go to where he is. We do the thing, then go our separate ways. You'd better not bail on me. I'm not doing this on my own. We agreed it was together."

Short sighed. "I *can't* do it on my own, you know that. It's one thing thinking about it, but being there by myself… He'd soon overpower me."

"Have you had any second thoughts this week?"

"Yeah. You?"

"Yeah. I thought about contacting The Brothers. They'd sort it for us."

"I know, but we wouldn't get the satisfaction."

"True."

"I want to feel the thing going in, know what I mean? Ever since I found out you… How could he *do* that to us?"

"Easily. He's a wanker. Has he suspected anything?"

"I don't think so. He's barely been at mine to be honest."

"Why do we women put up with it, eh?"

Lil could do with finding out the answer to that one. It sounded like these two were involved with the same bloke, or one of them used to be and the other was now. Lil didn't trusted men. They were arseholes.

Short straightened, as if she'd gone all uppity and indignant. "Well, I'm not putting up with it anymore. I wouldn't be doing this otherwise."

"It'll be better once he's gone."

"What if we get caught? There are so many cameras around these days."

"We won't. Why do you think he goes where he does of a night? He wouldn't be there if there was a chance he'd get nicked."

"And it's dark. Those streetlights have been broken. I walked past there today with Delaney."

"See? It'll be fine."

Then they sat in silence like last time, right through to the end of the washing and drying sessions. It was weird, but maybe they just wanted to sit there in the quiet with a kindred spirit. Other people had come in and sat, waiting, clothes tumbling round and round behind the big glass doors, so maybe that was another reason they hadn't nattered.

Ichabod got up to fold his dry laundry. He pushed it into a rucksack and put it on his back. Walked out. He'd likely wait in the dark and follow these two home. Their dryer cycle ended, and the pair got up to sort through whose stuff was whose, putting their piles in their respective black bags.

"I'll walk you as far as the Noodle," Short said.

The other woman nodded. "Cheers."

They left, and Lil turned around, watching them go past the window, their heads bent.

So they were going to kill someone tomorrow night, were they?

Lil smiled to herself.

Sometimes, killing them is the only way forward, my loves.

She should know. She'd done it twice.

To be continued in *Rhombus*
The Cardigan Estate 28